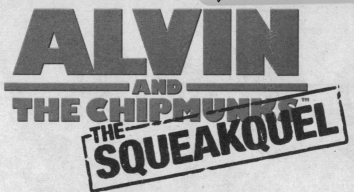

ALVIN AND THE CHIPMUNKS™: THE SQUEAKQUEL

THE JUNIOR NOVEL

HarperFestival is an imprint of HarperCollins Publishers.
Alvin and the Chipmunks: The Squeakquel: The Junior Novel

For information address HarperCollins Children's Books, a division of HarperCollins Publishers,
10 East 53rd Street, New York, NY 10022.
www.harpercollinschildrens.com
Library of Congress catalog card number: 2009935247
ISBN 978-0-06-184569-7
Typography by Fred Chao
09 10 11 12 13 LP/UG/CW   10 9 8 7 6 5 4 3 2 1

❖

First Edition

FOX 2000 PICTURES AND REGENCY ENTERPRISES PRESENT A BAGDASARIAN COMPANY PRODUCTION A BETTY THOMAS FILM "ALVIN AND THE CHIPMUNKS: THE SQUEAKQUEL"
ZACH LEVI DAVID CROSS AND JASON LEE AND JUSTIN LONG MATTHEW GRAY GUBLER JESSE McCARTNEY AMY POEHLER ANNA FARIS CHRISTINA APPLEGATE
COSTUME DESIGNER ALEXANDRA WELKER EXECUTIVE MUSIC PRODUCER ALI DEE THEODORE MUSIC SUPERVISOR JULIANNE JORDAN MUSIC BY DAVID NEWMAN ANIMATION SUPERVISOR CHRIS BAILEY FILM EDITOR MATTHEW FRIEDMAN
PRODUCTION DESIGNER MARCIA HINDS DIRECTOR OF PHOTOGRAPHY ANTHONY B. RICHMOND, ASC/BSC EXECUTIVE PRODUCERS KAREN ROSENFELT ARNON MILCHAN MICHELE IMPERATO STABILE STEVE WATERMAN
PRODUCED BY JANICE KARMAN ROSS BAGDASARIAN BASED UPON THE CHARACTERS "ALVIN AND THE CHIPMUNKS" CREATED BY ROSS BAGDASARIAN SCREENPLAY BY WILL McROBB AND CHRIS VISCARDI DIRECTED BY BETTY THOMAS

www.munkyourself.com

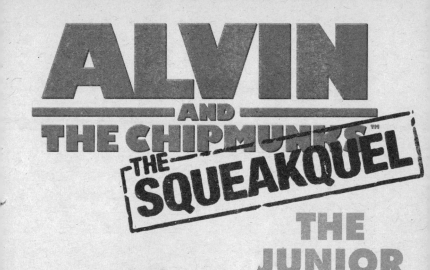

ALVIN
AND
THE CHIPMUNKS™
THE SQUEAKQUEL

THE
JUNIOR
NOVEL

Based upon the characters
Alvin and the Chipmunks
created by **Ross Bagdasarian**

Screenplay by **Will McRobb** &
Chris Viscardi
Adapted by **Perdita Finn**

HARPER FESTIVAL
An Imprint of HarperCollinsPublishers

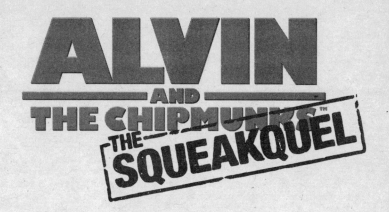

ALVIN
AND
THE CHIPMUNKS™
THE SQUEAKQUEL

THE JUNIOR NOVEL

chapter 1

In Paris, screaming fans crowded around an outdoor stage as the Eiffel Tower sparkled in the night. Alvin and the Chipmunks was the headlining act in a star-studded extravaganza to benefit VH1's *Save the Music*!

The crowd went wild as Alvin sang. He was hotter than ever! Simon, still wearing his glasses, riffed on his guitar. And little Theodore chirped and harmonized with his brothers. No one, anywhere, could resist these amazing singing and dancing chipmunk brothers.

In Tokyo teenage girls watched the concert on a massive outdoor TV. In Mexico tens of thousands of fans in a soccer stadium rocked to the music in front of a huge screen. Even in a faraway igloo, an Inuit family had their television tuned to the concert— and had to keep their sled dog from trying to attack the on-screen Chipmunks! All over the world people were listening to The Chipmunks—and loving them.

A guitar slung over his shoulder, Alvin flew over the crowd on an electrical wire. Fans reached up to grab him as he passed, but he was up too high. A girl wearing an "I'm Nuts for Simon" T-shirt rushed the stage. Alvin rocked the house! He was the star, the superstar! Even when he broke a guitar string from his furious playing, he didn't stop—just did a power slide into the wings, grabbed a new guitar from a roadie, and turned to head back onstage.

But he couldn't move. . . .

Dave had stepped on the cord of his electric guitar.

"Dave?" said Alvin, stunned. He motioned for Dave to move so he could continue the show.

"Take it easy out there," warned Dave. "There are rock 'n' roll legends out on that stage. You've gotta share the spotlight."

"You got it, Dave," said Alvin, not really listening. He was eager to get back in front of his fans. He tried to run off, but Dave still had his foot on his cord.

"I'm serious, Alvin," said Dave. "This is a charity benefit. It's not all about you."

"Sorry, Dave, can't hear you over the thousands of fans screaming my name." Turning away from him, Alvin yanked the cable from under Dave's foot and dashed back out to the concert. It was time for another showstopping solo!

Alvin jumped from the head of one famous rock star onto another, all the time wailing on his guitar. Finally, he took a mighty leap and landed on the top of a lighting tower. All eyes were on him.

"Alvin, please get down from there," shouted Dave from the wings of the theater.

The tower started to rock back and forth.

From the stage, Simon and Theodore exchanged nervous glances. Dave was worried, too. "Alvin! Listen to me!" he called.

For a moment Alvin stopped—and the scaffolding of the tower was still. But then he continued playing wildly.

"Alvin! I'm not kidding!" yelled Dave, more concerned than ever. The metal scaffolding of the tower started to teeter.

But Alvin just kept on rocking!

And that's all it took. The tower swayed back and forth, back and forth, and it began to topple over.

The fans screamed and ran. "Look out, Dave!" yelled little Theodore.

"ALVIN!!" yelled Dave one last time.

BOOM!

It was too late.

chapter 2

Sirens wailed. An ambulance raced down the narrow streets of Paris. It sped past a giant billboard promoting the *Save the Music* concert. All kinds of famous groups were listed, but the biggest billing was for Alvin and the Chipmunks. None of that mattered now. Dave, their friend who had rescued them and helped them with their music, was hurt.

By the time he was done being treated, Dave was wearing a neck brace. His leg was in traction. And his entire body was completely wrapped in bandages. A doctor gave him a shot.

"I want to talk to my boys," said Dave in a weak voice.

"I understand you, Monsieur Seville," said the French doctor. "But we just gave you a sedative that will take effect in sixty seconds."

Dave was firm. "I need to see my boys."

The Chipmunks had been waiting right outside the door, and the moment the nurse let them, they scurried over to Dave's bed.

"Oh, Dave!" gasped a stricken Theodore. "Are you in pain?"

"He won't be in about fifty seconds," reassured the nurse.

Alvin didn't know what to say. He felt terrible. He could barely look at Dave. "I'm really sorry," he managed to whisper.

"I'm going to be fine," said Dave, mustering his strength. "Don't worry about me. I'm just going to be stuck here for a while."

The nurse motioned to her watch. Dave needed to rest.

Dave nodded to her but continued to speak to his boys. He had to. He was like a father to them, and they needed his help and guidance. "The charity tour has been fun," he said. "But now it's over and it's time for us to go home. Until I'm out of here, I've arranged for my aunt Jackie to stay with you."

"Who's Aunt Jackie?" interrupted Alvin. He looked very concerned.

"The one who sends us those metal buckets with three kinds of popcorn for Christmas," Simon reminded him.

"Ooh! I like Aunt Jackie!" squealed Theodore. (Of course, what he really liked was popcorn—of any flavor.)

The nurse looked at her watch again. "Twenty seconds, Monsieur Seville."

Poor Dave. He was so tired. His speech was slowing down, and his words were beginning to slur. The sedative was starting to work. "I want you guys to have a normal childhood. You know, make friends, ride bikes, go to school . . ."

"School?" exclaimed all three chipmunks at the same time. They'd never been to school! Why did they need to go to school?

"Yes, school," said Dave as firmly as he could. The nurse was already counting down the seconds on her fingers until he would fall asleep. "Be good. No goofing around. No fighting. I need to know I can trust you guys. Simon, I'm putting you in charge. I'm counting . . . on . . . you. . . ."

Dave's eyelids fluttered shut. He was out. Alvin tried to wake him up. He was very upset. "Wait a minute! ¡Uno momento! Why is Simon in charge? Let me be in charge!"

Simon was smiling. He seemed very proud. "Dave's

7

counting on me," he announced.

Just at that moment, an official-looking woman in a suit came into the room. She was an airline representative. "I'm here to escort The Chipmunks home," she explained to the doctor.

"We're not leaving Dave!" insisted Alvin. Simon and Theodore crossed their arms and settled themselves onto the hospital bed. They wouldn't leave their friend either.

The nurse reached out to pick up Alvin and hand him to the airline representative, but Alvin made a run for it, accidentally landing on the switch that controlled Dave's hospital bed. Immediately, the bed began to fold up.

"You come back here right now," the nurse demanded.

But Alvin was frantic. Alvin jumped away from the nurse and hit another switch—this time sending the electric bed into all kinds of contortions. Simon and Theodore went flying across the room.

Smash! Theodore hit an IV stand, knocking it over.

Plunk! Simon landed in a bedpan.

The nurse lunged for Alvin again. Alvin leaped away—and landed on Dave's heart monitor, making it beep wildly. Alarm bells started ringing.

Dave's eyelids fluttered.

"Please, go. I beg you," insisted the doctor. "The more

stress you put on Monsieur Seville, the longer it will take him to recover."

"But Dave needs us!" said Alvin. "If we go, he'll be even more stressed out."

While the nurse was adjusting the electrical bed and setting it right, the doctor quietly took a syringe from a tray of medical supplies.

"You'll never take me!" yelled Alvin. "I'm not going anywhere without . . ."

The doctor stuck the needle into Alvin's rump. Immediately, Alvin's eyes began to roll back in his head. He weaved back and forth, but as he fell over, he called out, "Daaave!"

Alvin toppled over—right onto Dave's chest.

The doctor handed the quiet chipmunk to the airline representative. "I hope, for your sake, he stays asleep the entire flight."

Simon's head emerged from the bedpan. "You might want to give him an extra shot," he suggested. "Just in case."

chapter 3

Back at Jett Records in Los Angeles, executives were enjoying the success of their hottest group— Alvin and the Chipmunks! Each new hit brought more triumph to their label. On the eightieth floor, happy record producers hummed The Chipmunks' latest song while they helped themselves to coffee and muffins.

But deep in the dingy basement of the office tower lurked someone who was not so happy about The Chipmunks' success—their *old* manager, the one who had locked them in a cage, the villainous Ian Hawke.

Unshaven and bedraggled, Ian grabbed an old, used coffee filter from the Dumpster and hung it under a leaky water pipe. As coffee dripped into a battered mug, Ian listened to a tiny radio. And what was playing? Alvin and the Chipmunks, of course! He couldn't escape them anywhere.

Ian shook his head. He used to be a success! "I had fifteen cars," he said, remembering. "Seven maids. Courtside seats for Lakers games. Even my maids had courtside seats! Now look at me! Look at me!"

A whiskered rat turned his head and peered at Ian.

Ian was furious. He glared at the radio playing the latest Chipmunk hit. "It's all because of THEM!" He hurled the radio into the Dumpster, caught sight of a half-eaten muffin in the trash, and grabbed it. He dusted off the pencil shavings and took a thoughtful bite.

"I lost everything," he said, sighing. "Now I haunt the basement of Jett Records, hoping and praying that somewhere out there are more animals who can sing and dance." He noticed the rat and studied him carefully. "You don't sing, do you?"

The rat opened his mouth. Ian leaned forward, hopeful. Could it be?

In a flash, the rat chomped down on Ian's muffin and ran away with it!

"Hey!" screamed Ian.

He chased after the rat. With the muffin in his mouth, the rodent leaped into the Dumpster, and Ian dived in right behind him. He thrashed through the garbage hunting for the rat, but it was no good. He was completely and utterly defeated. He plopped down to catch his breath amid the trash and the cheerful voices of singing Chipmunks blaring from the radio he had just thrown away. It was as if they were taunting him! "I'll get you, Chipmunks!" vowed Ian.

Ian Hawke was ready for revenge.

chapter 4

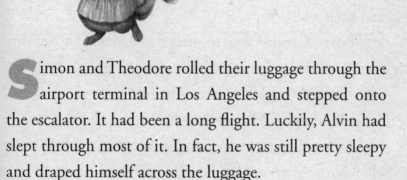

Simon and Theodore rolled their luggage through the airport terminal in Los Angeles and stepped onto the escalator. It had been a long flight. Luckily, Alvin had slept through most of it. In fact, he was still pretty sleepy and draped himself across the luggage.

Simon scanned the crowd. "How are we supposed to find Aunt Jackie?" he wondered aloud.

Theodore's little nose wiggled. He sniffed the air carefully. He could smell popcorn anywhere. "Follow me," he announced. He made his way through the jostling crowd. Bingo! He jumped onto a giant metal bucket, filled, he was sure, with three different delicious flavors. Next to the popcorn was Aunt Jackie.

She was an elderly lady with white hair, sitting in a wheelchair.

"Aunt Jackie!" chirped Theodore, Simon, and Alvin.

"Hello, dears!" said Aunt Jackie. And all three chipmunks leaped into her lap.

"So what's poppin', auntie baby?" asked Alvin, eyeing the popcorn tin Aunt Jackie was holding.

"There's plenty for everyone. But first give us a hug." The three chipmunks wrapped their arms around her. It had been a long trip.

"Boys, I want you to meet someone. This is my grandson, Toby." Aunt Jackie proudly gestured to the twentysomething boy standing behind her.

Behind the handles of the wheelchair was Toby Seville. He was wearing earphones and was lost in a video game. He hadn't even noticed The Chipmunks.

"Toby? Toby?" said Aunt Jackie, trying to get his attention. She finally reached up and grabbed his earbuds and pulled them out.

"Huh?" Toby said, and then he saw The Chipmunks. "Oh, yeah. Hey. I'm Toby." He laughed a bit and pointed at his game. "Protector of Princess Zelda."

Alvin gulped. The Chipmunks exchanged a look of concern that seemed to say, "Okaaay."

"Toby's living with me," explained Aunt Jackie, "while he decides what to do with his life. As far as I can tell that

14

means going *pew pew* with his thumbs all day." She used her fingers to mime the action of playing a video game.

Toby stuck up this thumbs proudly. "Hey, respect these thumbs. They just wiped out an army of evil." He started to push Aunt Jackie's wheelchair toward the exit.

"Toby!" said Aunt Jackie. "Don't forget The Chipmunks' bags."

"Right. Sorry," said Toby. As he turned to pick up the little bags, he accidentally bumped into the wheelchair. It started to roll toward a long flight of stairs.

"Toby! Toby! Tobeeeeeeeeeeee!" yelled Aunt Jackie.

Simon squealed. "Runaway auntie!" The wheelchair was out of control!

"Abandon ship!" commanded Alvin.

The Chipmunks jumped off—just before the wheelchair and Aunt Jackie bounced down the flight of stairs into a traffic jam of luggage carts.

The Chipmunks cringed as they listened to the screech and screams of the collision.

Luckily, an ambulance arrived quickly to bring Aunt Jackie to the hospital. While the paramedics strapped her to the gurney, poor Toby looked on. "Is she going to be okay?" he asked them. His face was white.

"Don't worry about me," reassured Aunt Jackie. "I'll

be home in no time."

Behind her back, one of the paramedics shook his head. "I wouldn't be so sure," he said.

"It was an accident, I swear," said Toby to The Chipmunks.

Alvin looked at Toby. He knew a thing or two about accidents. "I've been there, buddy," he said sympathetically.

chapter 5

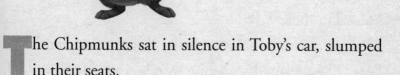

The Chipmunks sat in silence in Toby's car, slumped in their seats.

"So, I guess you'll be taking care of us now?" questioned Theodore in a nervous voice.

"That's a comforting thought," whispered Alvin. His whiskers twitched.

"Um, I guess," said Toby as he loaded the broken wheelchair into the car. "But I can totally do this. No problem." The Chipmunks did not look reassured as Toby continued. "I mean, I took care of my cat, 'til he ran away. But I still see him on the street sometimes. He hisses at me and his hair shoots straight up, but we're still tight."

Alvin looked worried. Simon looked shocked. Theodore looked panicked.

"I'm not gonna try to be Dave," said Toby, thinking he understood their concern. "Dave's gone."

Tears welled up in Theodore's eyes.

Toby couldn't help himself. He kept making things worse. "I mean, like, for now," he tried. "I mean, he's completely coming back. But for now I'm gonna be in Dave's room, keeping his bed warm. I'm going to be doin' what I'm doin'. I got my own stuff. You're not even gonna know I'm there."

This wasn't what the little chipmunks wanted to hear. They wanted someone to take care of them, look out for things, and make sure they were okay. "We're supposed to know you're there, that's the idea," said Simon.

"Yeah. No. I mean, you're totally gonna know I'm there," backtracked Toby. "It's just, I'm not gonna be all . . . 'I'm Mr. Expert, I know everything. You do this. You do that.' That's the way my dad sounds."

But that's what The Chipmunks wanted. A dad. Dave. Horrified, they didn't say another word.

Toby set the smashed popcorn tin on the seat next to the boys. The Chipmunks looked even more upset. Toby settled into the driver's seat, gunned the engine, and peeled out of the parking lot.

"Okay, let's do this!" Toby announced with forced cheerfulness.

Flattened against the backseat, The Chipmunks sat stunned. What were they going to do?

Elsewhere at the airport, a large jet touched down on a runway. When it came to a stop at the terminal, the cargo door opened ever so slightly. Three little faces peeked out. They were chipmunks. Girl chipmunks.

"We made it, girls!" exclaimed Brittany. "Los Angeles. I can't believe we're really here." The wind blew her fur into her eyes, and she brushed it away with her paws.

"Now we just need to find Jett Records," said Jeanette.

"I got it all figured out," said Eleanor. "We'll be there before ten tomorrow morning, guaranteed."

They were quite a team. A *singing* team. Britanny. Jeanette. Eleanor.

The Chipettes had arrived in L.A.

chapter 6

Theodore couldn't stop thinking about Dave. He sat on his little bed with his name on it making him a get-well card. Glue, crayons, and paper were scattered all over.

"We're going to be just fine, Theodore," reassured Simon. "Don't you worry."

Theodore poured more glitter onto the giant card. "Maybe my get-well card will help Dave get home faster."

Alvin examined his work. "You know what this puppy needs? A touch more glitter. Dave loves the sparkly stuff." He poured a huge bottle all over the card—and the bed. "That should do it," he decided. "Who's hungry?"

Alvin left Theodore to try and fix his card and Simon to clean up the mess. He went into the kitchen. He hummed to himself as he opened empty cupboard after empty cupboard. There was just no food in the house.

But at last he found one lone bag. Cheese balls. Yum.

Alvin bit the bag. He pulled at it. He stomped on it and tried to pop it open. Finally, in a frenzy, he wrapped his arms around it like a wrestler, and it opened with a gentle *poof.*

Simon, Theodore, and Toby ran into the room.

"What's going on in here?" asked Toby.

Sheepishly Alvin held up the plastic bag of cheese balls. He held it out invitingly to Toby. "Cheese ball?" he offered.

"Alvin, I'm trying to focus," said Toby angrily. "The princess is surrounded. My army is gone. I've got a lot going on right now." Toby had been in his room playing his video game.

"Can we help?" asked Simon eagerly.

"Nothing personal, guys. But this is no time for amateurs," said Toby seriously.

"We can play Monopoly," offered Theodore. "We play Monopoly with Dave all the time."

Toby couldn't hide his lack of interest. "Love to, guys," he said. "But the Twilight Realm isn't going to save itself. So, first day with the Tobester. Fun, right?"

The Chipmunks didn't say a word. The apartment felt so empty without Dave.

"I know. It was boring," said Toby. "But tomorrow is another day." He headed back to his room and all the monsters he had to fight on his video game. Theodore looked really sad.

Simon wrapped an arm around his brother protectively. "We don't need Toby to have fun," he said.

"No, we don't," agreed Alvin, brightening. "Boys, right this way. . . . This way to the fun zone. Fun is my middle name."

Alvin grabbed the junk food and headed over to the bladeless food processor. His brothers followed, and soon they were all lying on their backs in the plastic bowl eating cheese balls. When they started to sing "You Spin Me 'Round," Alvin got an idea. He reached up and pulled a string he'd attached to a coffee mug and a meat-tenderizing mallet. The mallet fell and hit the on button of the food processor.

Now The Chipmunks weren't just singing about spinning, they were *really* spinning—and pretty fast, too!

The faster they spun, the wobblier they got and the woozier they sang! Finally, they couldn't even hold on anymore. One by one they let go—and were whipped out of the bowl and across the room.

They ended up dangling from the metal hangers of a potrack.

"Do you know what Dave would say if he were here right now?" Alvin was so dizzy that his words were slurred.

"Alvin!!" shouted Theodore—sounding almost like Dave.

"Not bad," said Alvin. "But it needs to come more from the belly."

Together the brothers began perfecting their yells. "ALVIN!!" they all called.

Just then the phone rang.

Alvin and Simon hopped down off the rack effortlessly and hit the speakerphone. Theodore tried to wriggle free.

"Boys, it's me!" Dave called over the phone.

"Dave!" responded all three chipmunks happily.

"I guess since you answered the phone you haven't burned the house down yet," Dave said, relieved.

With a loud *clunk*, Theodore fell off the potrack onto the floor.

"What was that?" asked Dave. He sounded concerned.

Simon gestured to Theodore to be quiet. "Don't stress him out," he whispered to Alvin. Simon knew Dave needed his rest so he could get better.

"Uh," stuttered Alvin. "That was . . . um . . . Aunt Jackie. She's making us a tasty five-course meal."

"Can I talk to her?" asked Dave.

Alvin looked frantically at Simon. Simon tried to stall. "She's . . . uh . . ."

"Sleeping!" blurted out Theodore triumphantly.

Simon slapped his forehead. That wasn't the answer he was hoping for.

Dave seemed to suspect that something was up, too. "I thought you said she was making dinner."

But before he could say anything else, Toby walked into the room and Alvin yelled at the speakerphone, "Relax and get better, Dave. Gotta go!"

Back in his hospital room, though, Dave knew that something was not right. "Alvin, I'm not joking."

"Get well soon!" said Alvin.

Dave's heart monitor was beeping faster and faster. "ALVIN!!"

Alvin hung up the phone. "Boy, nobody yells my name better than Dave," he said, smiling.

chapter 7

That night The Chipmunks abandoned their beds and snuggled together in Dave's big leather chair. Alvin slept soundly as always, happily mumbling songs. Simon talked in his sleep, whispering the answers to math problems. But Theodore, covered in glitter and glue, tossed and turned on top of the card he'd made. Across it were written the words, *Dave, come home soon.*

All at once, Theodore bolted upright in the chair, his little black eyes wide with terror. He crept out of the chair and into the bedroom. He hopped up onto the bed where Toby was still awake.

"Sorry," apologized Theodore, looking down at his paws.

"No, that's okay. What is it?" asked Toby.

Theodore's voice was very quiet. "I had a nightmare," he whispered.

"I hate the nightmares," said Toby, surprisingly sympathetic. "What was it?"

"I dreamed we didn't have a family anymore," said Theodore sadly.

Toby's face softened. "Aww, Theodore," he said, reaching out a hand. "That couldn't happen. You guys are tight. Nothing could ever separate you. Unless, like, an eagle swooped out of the sky . . ."

Theodore, who had just started to relax, jumped up in alarm, a look of terror on his face.

Toby hastened to reassure him. ". . . which couldn't happen ever, so how could it happen?" He added in a firm voice. "It couldn't."

But it was too late. Theodore had jumped off the bed and was backing out of the room, more frightened than ever.

But Toby didn't notice. "That went well," he said, complimenting himself. He settled back to into bed and fell instantly asleep.

chapter 8

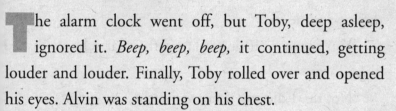

The alarm clock went off, but Toby, deep asleep, ignored it. *Beep, beep, beep,* it continued, getting louder and louder. Finally, Toby rolled over and opened his eyes. Alvin was standing on his chest.

"What are you doing?" Toby mumbled. He was tired and grouchy.

Alvin pointed at the small clock. "There's something wrong with this clock," he said. "It's making noises. I can't sleep."

Toby smiled sleepily. "That's the point. That's an alarm clock. It helps you wake up early."

"Why would we ever want to wake up early?" asked Alvin, confused.

"For school," said Toby, remembering. "We have to be there by eight."

"In the *morning*?" questioned Alvin, stunned. He couldn't believe it.

"Look," said Toby. "I don't like getting up this early either. But we're in this together. The sooner you get to school, the sooner I get to come home and go back to sleep."

Alvin didn't think that that was very fair, but before he knew it, they were all in Toby's car headed to their first day of school. Unfortunately, Toby didn't plan on helping the boys settle in.

"You mean, you don't stay with us at school?" asked Theodore.

"No, no. I did my time. Seriously."

"But school is fun, right?" asked Theodore.

Toby laughed out loud like that was the stupidest thing he'd ever heard. He stopped only when he noticed how puzzled and worried The Chipmunks buckled in beside him looked.

"It's fun-ish."

Toby didn't stick around after he'd dropped off The Chipmunks. The moment they closed the car door, he sped away from the school as fast as he could.

The high school was big, and The Chipmunks felt little. Huge steps, hundreds of them, led up to the front door. Enormous teenagers were everywhere—lounging around, gossiping. Each of The Chipmunks took a deep breath and headed toward the stairs. This was it.

Alvin ran up the stairs almost effortlessly. "That wasn't so bad," he said cheerfully when he got to the top. Simon arrived behind him a little more slowly. It took him a moment to catch his breath. But poor Theodore just couldn't make it. By the time he'd reached the last step, he was utterly exhausted. Alvin and Simon had to reach down and hoist him up over the final ledge.

At that exact moment, the school bell rang and a stampede of students rushed past the little chipmunks. They dodged shoes, bouncing basketballs, wheeled backpacks, and even whizzing skateboards.

"Don't mind us!" shouted Alvin, trying to keep from being stepped on.

Theodore, who barely came up to the ankles of all those passing legs, tried to wave at the kids as they whizzed by. "Hi, I'm Theodore," he said again and again, hoping to make a friend.

But before anyone could see him, much less answer him, an eagle-costumed skateboarder sped right toward him. The teenager screamed at the top of his lungs. "Go, Eagles!"

Theodore screamed in fear.

The clueless kid flew right over Theodore's tail and careened down the stairs. Simon and Alvin rushed over to see if Theodore was okay.

A little shell-shocked, Theodore staggered back into place. "This isn't very fun . . . ish." He stopped himself from being completely negative as the high heel of a very professional woman stepped beside him. She was really tall and a little scary looking. She seemed important.

"You must be our new students. I'm Dr. Rubin, the principal."

"And we're The Chipmunks!" announced Theodore sweetly. Beside him, Simon and Alvin gave the principal their cutest smiles.

But Dr. Rubin was not impressed. "That explains the fur and the bushy tails," she said icily.

Reluctantly, the three chipmunks followed the principal. Theodore held on to his tail to keep it close. In the hallway outside a classroom, Dr. Rubin stopped and gave The Chipmunks a stern lecture.

"I hope you don't expect any special treatment," she began. She wasn't smiling. "You may be famous, but here, in the hallowed halls of West Eastman High School you are just ordinary students like everyone else." She nodded briskly and opened the door to the classroom.

Nervously, The Chipmunks entered the room.

Class had not yet begun. A pretty, young teacher sat at her desk, and in the back of the room a gaggle of girls crowded around two boys in varsity jackets. Ryan said dramatically, "There was like a minute left, and we were down by two, and I'm like, 'Coach, I don't care if my leg is broken. Put me in, I can win this.'"

"I never get tired of this story," said Becca, a pretty girl.

"Shh," said her friend Valentina. "Let Ryan finish."

"So," continued Ryan. "I hobble out, barely able to stand, knowing it's all up to me . . . Did I mention my leg was broken?"

The girls were riveted.

"I had one guy on my broken leg," bragged Ryan. "Two guys hanging off my back, but I wouldn't go down. Somehow I threw the ball to the . . ."

"The Chipmunks!" the girls exclaimed breathlessly. They left Ryan's side and swarmed around The Chipmunks.

"Hello, ladies," said Alvin, pleased.

Theodore smiled bashfully. "Hi, I'm Theodore." He extended his paw to one of the girls.

"Hi, I'm Theodore," he said to another, and he was

just about to open his mouth again, when Simon threw a paw over it.

"His name's Theodore," he said to a dark-haired girl. She laughed out loud and Simon smiled.

But Alvin stole the show—as always. He leaped up, kissed Becca's hand, and announced in French, "Alvin. *Enchanté*."

The girl blushed.

Ryan, the boy in the varsity jacket, was not happy. He turned away from the girls and The Chipmunks to his jock buddy. "I think someone's gonna have to knock those guys down to size," he said.

"That shouldn't be hard," said his friend Xander. "They're only eight inches tall."

Ryan glared at Xander and then looked over to The Chipmunks.

But The Chipmunks didn't notice Ryan. They were paying attention to the throng of girls surrounding them. Suddenly, The Chipmunks thought school wasn't going to be so bad after all.

chapter 9

Little did The Chipmunks realize that across town at Jett Records an old enemy was plotting his revenge.

Wearing a tattered silk robe, Ian brushed his teeth—in a fountain in front of the building.

Just as he spit onto the pavement, a delivery truck pulled up to the curb. The driver got out and carried a large crate filled with letters and packages toward the office building. One of the envelopes, though, was wriggling. Without the driver realizing it, the package twitched right out of the crate onto the sidewalk and wobbled across the pavement.

The furry striped head of a little chipmunk burst through the envelope.

One by one, The Chipettes crawled out of the package.

Brittany noticed Ian by the fountain almost at once. "Oh, my gosh," she exclaimed. "It's him. Ian Hawke!"

The small, chirpy voice caught Ian's attention. It was familiar, somehow.

"That voice. I can't get it out of my head!"

He spun around, and there, right in front of him, were three chipmunks. He couldn't believe it.

"Hello. What have we here?" he asked, looking down.

"We have a Brittany," said the chipmunk who had approached him. "And this is my sister Eleanor."

Another of the girl chipmunks came over. "Hello, sir," she said very politely and held out her paw for Ian to shake. Ian wiped his hand on his robe and took hers.

The third chipmunk introduced herself with a shy wave. "I'm Jeanette," she said. "Although sometimes I feel more like an Olivia, and other times . . ."

"Anyway, we're The Chipettes," interrupted Brittany, stepping in front of her sister. "And we'd be honored if you would represent us."

Ian couldn't believe his ears. It had been a long time since he had had music clients, especially chipmunks. But he still knew how to use his charm. "You girls are making me blush," he enthused.

"You made Alvin and the Chipmunks stars. We want to be stars, too."

Ian narrowed his eyes. "Before we get too girly and

giggly, please tell me you can sing."

Brittany held up a finger to indicate she and her sisters would just be a minute. The three chipmunk girls huddled together, whispering, their tails intertwined. They were an impressive team.

Brittany began to count off. "One. Two. Three . . ."

But just in case they really could sing, Ian stopped them with a big, oily smile. "Why don't we continue this in my penthouse office?" They started for the main entrance, but Ian stopped them.

"No, no. Come with me, to the exclusive, supersecret *artists only* back staircase." He motioned for them to follow him into the alley.

It was a long, long climb up the back stairs, but finally Ian brought The Chipettes out onto the rooftop of the Jett Records building. It was furnished with all kinds of junky furniture found in the trash and leftover luxuries from Ian's old life as a top manager. There was a tropical fish tank, gold records, and even a putting strip from his successful years, now long gone.

But all The Chipettes really noticed was the amazing view of Los Angeles spreading out around them. "Wow!" said Brittany, pointing at the famous letters on the hillside. "It's the Hollywood sign."

"I thought you might like the view," said Ian.

Eleanor went to sit down, but noticed how dirty the chair was. With her tail, she dusted it off. Brittany, seeing the clean spot, grabbed the seat before her sister could. Eleanor rolled her eyes.

Ian pretended not to notice and continued to act like the big manager he used to be. "So, tell me every little thing about yourselves."

"Well," Brittany chirped, "we're from a small town, population three hundred, and . . ."

Ian interrupted her before she could continue. There was only one thing he wanted to know. "That's great. Let's get back to the singing." He didn't want to waste his time if they were no good.

After a brief huddle, The Chipettes broke into song. And what a song it was. They were amazing! Mind-blowing! As good as Alvin and his brothers. Better maybe. Ian couldn't believe it.

When they finished, he took a moment to catch his breath. "Who just became the number one Chipettes fan in the whole dang world?" He raised his own hand, smiling. "Ian Hawke, that's who."

"So when can we meet The Chipmunks?" asked Eleanor eagerly.

Ian paused, rubbing his hands together. "That's an excellent question. And the excellent answer is . . . I don't actually represent The Chipmunks anymore."

Brittany's dark eyes widened. "What happened?"

Ian smiled, trying to look relaxed. "Classic tale," he lied. "Sweet guys when they had nothing, and then when I made them rock stars, it all changed. They turned on me like bad cheese."

Jeanette couldn't believe it. "That's terrible!"

Ian shook his head and sighed. "I treated Alvin like my own son, and he spit on me. He literally gathered saliva in his chipmunk cheeks and let me have it. And don't get me started on Simon!"

"Theodore, too?" asked Eleanor, aghast.

"It's the cuddly ones you have to watch out for," said Ian, neglecting to tell the girls about how he had actually treated The Chipmunks—giving them too much caffeine, never letting them rest, locking them in a pet carrier. "But enough about those has-beens. They're over. Done. A novelty act. Chipmunks who can sing? Tired. But *girl* chipmunks who can sing? Fasten your seat belts!"

The Chipettes exchanged excited glances. Ian Hawke was going to make them stars!

chapter 10

Back at school, Alvin, Simon, and Theodore were enjoying lunch in the cafeteria—surrounded by Becca and a crowd of attentive girls.

Alvin was wowing them with stories about all the stars he'd met. ". . . So here's the thing about this rapper. He's the world's biggest collector of Alvin plush dolls. A lot of people don't know that."

Simon was having a cozy conversation with another girl. "Yeah, Dave put me in charge," he was explaining. "I'm kind of the 'big picture' guy."

Theodore had a different way of making an impression. With a hop and a smile, he jumped onto the end of a fork, launching a tater tot into the air—and caught it in his mouth. Becca beamed. "You are Theo-adorable," she gushed.

Ryan passed by their table just in time to hear this, so he "accidentally" knocked into Alvin's lunch tray. All the food fell on the ground.

"Oh, I am *soooo* sorry," said Ryan sarcastically.

Alvin shrugged. He didn't care. He was having too much fun with the girls to worry about food. "No harm done," he said to Ryan.

"Not yet," muttered Ryan. "Girls, please. A private conference here." He motioned for them to leave and took a seat next to The Chipmunks.

"Listen up, rock stars," warned Ryan in a menacing voice. "If you talk to those girls again, you're dead. If you look at those girls again, you're dead. If you even think about those girls again . . ." He stopped midsentence and studied The Chipmunks' faces suspiciously. "Are you thinking about them?"

"I am now," joked Alvin. Ryan didn't scare him at all.

"That's it. You're dead," said Ryan.

chapter 11

The Chipmunks were little, but they could run fast when they needed to. Which was a good thing. Because Ryan and his buddies were chasing them down the hall.

Finally, the jocks got Alvin into a corner and surrounded him.

But before they could grab him, Alvin scurried between their legs, jumped on their backs, grabbed the waistbands of their boxers, and gave them wedgies!

Poor Theodore wasn't so lucky. He was chased toward a giant statue of the school's eagle mascot. This totally freaked him out and sent him hiding in an office. At first, the bullies couldn't find him. But then one of the boys pointed to a suspicious lump on top of the copy machine—a piece of paper under the cover with a tail. One of the boys pushed a button, and the machine whirred into action. A moment later a copy emerged from the paper tray. It showed Theodore—flattened and frightened.

Meanwhile, Simon was hanging out in the bathroom. Literally. Ryan and Xander had grabbed him by his tail and were holding him upside down over the toilet. Ryan flushed. Xander dropped the chipmunk. Ryan and Xander couldn't stop laughing as they headed back to the hallway.

Alvin arrived just in the nick of time and managed to lower his tail to Simon. Simon fought his way out of the swirling water and grabbed the tail while Alvin pulled. Simon lay on the tiles of the bathroom floor, catching his breath. That had been really, really scary.

"I'll be right back," said Alvin to his recovering brother. Alvin was mad.

He strode purposefully to the door, but he couldn't move. Simon had stopped him by stepping on his tail.

"We won't solve anything with violence," said Simon, concerned.

They heard menacing laughter from the hallway. Ryan and Xander were lurking right outside the door.

Simon and Alvin tiptoed over to the door and peeked out.

Ryan and Xander were teasing Theodore, poking him and laughing—"This one's got some serious junk in the trunk"—but a moment later they weren't. Two wild-eyed, sharp-clawed chipmunks attacked them. No one made fun of their little brother. No one.

chapter 12

The Chipmunks waited outside the principal's office. They were in big trouble and they knew it. Theodore had stretched his hoodie way down so that it covered his knees.

"Simon, does this make me look thinner?" he whispered.

Simon patted him on the pack. "You look good," he reassured Theodore. "Those guys are just jerks."

Ryan and Xander slunk by the door where The Chipmunks were sitting. Their clothes were shredded from head to toe. As they passed, Alvin bared his teeth and growled at them. The boys jumped back in fright and ran as fast as they could down the hall.

Dr. Rubin, stern and unsmiling, opened the door to her office. Without a word, she motioned to The

Chipmunks to come in and waited until they were seated in front of her desk before beginning to speak.

She took a deep breath. "You threatened to climb inside of him and build a nest," she said to Simon.

"I'm sorry. That was out of line," Simon apologized. "I'm not even sure that's physically possible."

Alvin snickered, and Dr. Rubin shook her head. "Gentlemen, I understand your parental situation is, shall we say, unsettled. But in this school we use our words, not our claws." She paused. "I should suspend the three of you."

"Please do!" begged Alvin eagerly. It had been only one day, but he hated school already.

Dr. Rubin frowned at Alvin. "Instead, I have a better idea."

The Chipmunks began grumbling among themselves, but Dr. Rubin ignored them and continued speaking. "Because of budget cutbacks, we're in jeopardy of losing our beloved music program."

"That's awful!" said Simon sincerely.

"There is one ray of hope, however," said Dr. Rubin. "Every year the district sponsors a music competition. Each school enters a band to represent them, and the winner collects twenty-five thousand dollars. If we win,

44

we can save our program."

Simon nodded. "And you want us to perform?"

"I didn't think you were a fan," grumbled Alvin.

"I'm not," said Dr. Rubin. "Nothing personal, but the sound of three woodland creatures singing does not exactly float my proverbial boat." The phone rang and Dr. Rubin excused herself while she reached for it. As she did so, the sleeve of her jacket pulled back on her arm, revealing a tattoo. An "Alvin and the Chipmunks" tattoo!

"Hello?" said Dr. Rubin into the phone receiver.

The Chipmunks stared at the tattoo. Could Dr. Rubin be a secret fan? Dr. Rubin noticed their little black eyes all looking at her arm. "I have to go," she said quickly and hung up the phone.

"Busted!" squealed Alvin, delighted.

Dr. Rubin blushed. She got up from her desk and carefully closed the window blinds. She checked to see that the door was shut. "Promise me you won't tell anyone," she begged The Chipmunks. "A principal has a certain image to uphold. If any of the faculty found out that . . ." An enormous smile spread across her face. She gazed at The Chipmunks with an expression of absolute adoration. "I cannot believe that you are actually in my office. I have all your CDs. I even saw you play last year in Denver." She lowered her voice to a whisper. "I told the school board I was going to a conference."

Dr. Rubin held out her arm so The Chipmunks could now get a good look at her tattoo. "It was a pretty wild night," she explained. "Can you imagine if the school board found out about it?

"So what do you say? Will you represent the school? Please say yes," she begged.

"I don't know," said Alvin, but he was smiling. "We're pretty busy getting beat up all day."

But Theodore couldn't hold back his excitement. "What do you say, guys?" He wrapped an arm around each of his brothers. "One for all and three for one!"

"Close enough," Simon said, smiling.

"Go, Eagles!" exclaimed Dr. Rubin.

"Eagles?" screamed Theodore in a sudden panic. "Where?"

Dr. Rubin laughed and ruffled him on the head reassuringly. Her music program would be saved—and by her favorite band ever!

chapter 13

Ian and The Chipettes stood outside a building in the center of the city. A sign high up in one of the apartment windows read, NEW LOFTS: MODELS AVAILABLE NOW. It was just what Ian needed—an empty apartment that he could pretend was his. That way The Chipettes wouldn't realize how down on his luck he really was.

He opened the front door of the building for the three girl chipmunks and led them to the elevator as if he lived there. The elevator door opened—and out walked a very handsome Chihuahua, the canine star of a recent movie. The dog gave Brittany a very flirtatious look.

"Is that *him*? From the movie?" Brittany couldn't believe it! She was really in Hollywood now.

"A lot of big stars live here," said Ian casually.

"I'm going to get his autograph," squealed Brittany.

Ian held up his hand and stopped her. "*You're* the star, Brittany. You don't get autographs. You give autographs."

They took the elevator up and up and got off near the top of the building. As quickly as he could and without The Chipettes noticing, Ian ripped a sign off the wall that said, MODEL B LOFTS THIS WAY. He stuffed it into his pocket. He walked over to an apartment door and tried to open it. Then he made a big show of patting his pockets. "Oh, darn it! Darn it to heck!"

"What's wrong?" asked Jeanette.

"I left my keys back at the office," Ian lied. "Don't worry. It'll only take us three hours to get back with all the traffic."

The girls groaned. They'd already done so much traveling in one day!

"Wait! Hold on!" said Ian dramatically. "Maybe one of you could climb in through the mail slot and open the door." He glanced around. "Quickly. Like real fast." That had been his idea all along, of course.

"I'll do it!" volunteered Eleanor instantly.

She scurried up the door as if it were a tree and pushed open the mail slot. Unfortunately, her bottom was a little bigger than the opening and she made it only halfway. She was too big to get through. Ian pulled her out by her tail.

"Not quick enough. Jeanette, maybe you could . . . ," he suggested to Eleanor's smaller sister.

Jeanette dived in and within moments they were all inside the apartment.

Ian reached around in the dark apartment, found the switch, and flipped on the lights. It was a spectacular loft-style apartment. A movie star's home. The furniture was expensive and tasteful. There were large windows overlooking the bright lights of Los Angeles. The girls rushed to look out at the city. They were overwhelmed. This is what they had dreamed of back in the country.

Ian was overwhelmed, too. He was back on top—and he'd show Alvin and the Chipmunks. "It's not much, but I call it home," he said, sighing.

chapter 14

Theodore was home and snuggled up in front of the television watching his favorite program. Simon was busy picking up around the apartment. Toby had left stuff everywhere.

The narrator of the meerkat show was describing how the Whiskers family had been chased out of their territory and now had to find a new place to live. Theodore felt sad. He missed Dave so much. He patted the sofa, inviting Simon to watch with him. "The Whiskers are digging their new home. Just like when we buried Dave in the sand at the beach."

"That sounds nice," Simon said. He settled in beside Theodore, but just as he was leaning back against a blanket draped over the sofa, he heard a suspicious crunching sound. He lifted the blanket and discovered a hard, stale, moldy taco. He shook his head, muttering to himself. "Toby!" That guy didn't take responsibility for anything.

As usual, Toby was playing video games—and Alvin had joined him for virtual bowling. Alvin psyched himself up. He cracked his neck and knuckles, did a couple deep knee bends, wound up his arms. Toby was getting impatient. "While we're still young," he complained, tapping his foot.

"Hey!" said Alvin. "You can't rush greatness!" He smiled.

"Go, Alvin!" Simon yelled. "Take this clown down."

"Yeah, go, Alvin, go, Alvin. Go!" chanted Theodore.

"Rough crowd!" said Toby.

"Maybe you'd have more fans if you cleaned the house once in a while," said Simon.

"Wow!" said Toby, surprised at how mad Simon was at him. "Is this going to be one of those *blame* households?"

Alvin got ready to throw the imaginary ball down the lane. He raised his arm, ran forward, and let go—of the controller. It hurled through the air and smashed right into the flat-screen television. *Kapowee!*

Everyone froze in shock.

Finally, Simon cleared his throat. "Just a suggestion.

Let's not tell Dave about this until he gets home."

"Or never," muttered Alvin, stricken with shame.

"Never works for me," agreed Theodore.

Alvin forced a smile. "So, we're good, right, Tobester?"

Toby wasn't smiling. "No," he said bluntly.

"C'mon on, man, cut us a break," begged Alvin. "This day has been bad enough already."

Toby flopped down on the couch. "Problems at school?" he guessed.

"Not really," said Simon. "Unless you consider getting your head dunked in the toilet a problem."

"Ouch," said Toby, wincing. "Nothing worse than getting the swirlie." And he knew what he was talking about. The same thing had happened to him in high school. But he didn't want to admit that to The Chipmunks. "At least that's what I've heard," he added, covering his slip.

But Simon had seen the flash of emotions across his face. "Toby, what was school like for you?" he asked pointedly.

Toby had an instant memory of going to the water fountain and discovering that it was booby-trapped— after it had sprayed the front of his pants, making it look like he'd had an accident. Everyone laughed at him. Everyone, that is, except Julie. He had such a crush on Julie. But he could never have gone out with a girl like her. He got teased too much. Kids put signs on his back that said PINCH ME, and, unaware, he'd walked around all day getting pinched and poked, even by that stupid eagle mascot. It hurt just to remember it.

The worst thing, though, had been gym class. Killerball. It was like dodgeball, only ten times worse. Once, Julie had walked by the gym and waved at him. That was all it took. He froze. And every kid hurled their balls at him at the same time, knocking him down to the floor—right in front of the girl he liked.

"Toby?" said Alvin.

"What?" said Toby, emerging from his memories.

"What was school like for you?" asked Simon again.

Toby shook off the troubling memories and lied. "In a word, *awesome*," he told The Chipmunks. "Not like some people who are all 'Oh, high school was like prison because I got stuffed in a locker all the time and no girl would talk to me and, like, I'm sorry if I smell.'"

The Chipmunks couldn't really follow what Toby was saying. Was he describing what had happened to him or someone else?

"I guess you could say I was one of those 'Most Likely to Succeed' types," lied Toby.

"Is that why you live with your grandma?" asked Alvin innocently.

"And never leave the house?" added Simon.

They had hit a nerve.

Toby stood up and pointed at the door. "Out," he told The Chipmunks. "Out."

chapter 15

Back in Paris, Dave was still confined to his hospital
bed. He couldn't stop thinking about his chipmunks,
and it was almost too much for him when a nurse brought
him Theodore's giant get-well card. "Are these guys sweet or
what?" he said to the nurse. "They're good kids. I just have
to learn to trust them."

He opened up the card and a shower of glitter poured
out—right onto his face. He choked. He coughed. He
thrashed around. And he accidentally hit the control
button for his automatic hospital bed. It started closing up
with Dave inside it! His heart monitor started beeping. The
nurse rushed over. What a mess!

"Alvin!" yelled Dave from inside the bed. Even from
thousands of miles away, those little chipmunks could
make big trouble!

The alarm clock beeped again. It was morning and time for school.

"Alvin!" yelled Toby from the bedroom. "Turn that thing off!"

But the beeping continued.

"Alvin!" yelled Toby again. Fuming, he pulled himself out of bed and stomped out of the bedroom over to the chair where The Chipmunks liked to sleep. It was empty. Confused, Toby turned off the alarm and looked around. He couldn't see The Chipmunks anywhere. "Guys? Where are you? Come on. You've got to go to school."

He looked in the kitchen. They weren't there. Then he looked in the bathroom. They weren't there. "Boys, this isn't funny," he shouted at them, wherever they were. He listened. He thought he'd heard a muffled sound. He had! Someone was calling on a cell phone from inside the toilet!

Toby lifted the lid—and there were The Chipmunks, clinging to the rim and dangling above the water. Alvin was whispering on the phone. "Hello? Humane Society? I need help. A man is chasing us. He wants to take us to a terrible place . . ."

"Out," ordered Toby.

"Have a heart," begged Simon, desperate.

"Dave wants you to go to school," said Toby. "So you're going."

"Yeah," argued Alvin. "Well, don't worry about picking us up at three. We'll be dead by noon!"

Toby sighed. "Guys, trust me. The second day is never as bad as the first."

chapter 16

The second day didn't start as badly as the first—it was worse!

The students were playing Killerball in the gym, and The Chipmunks were getting bombarded. Kids in shorts hurled a blizzard of red rubber balls at them. They jumped. They dived. They flipped. It was insane! It was terrifying.

"Glasses!" shrieked Simon, pointing at his face. "Guy with glasses!"

Boom!

Simon was the first to get hit by a ball and go down. He was out!

Boom!

Theodore was next! "Call the nurse!" he begged comically.

THE CHIPMUNKS

THEODORE

BRITTANY

Only Alvin remained. He somersaulted and rolled, dashed and turned, but he could hold out for only so long. Ryan whipped a ball at Alvin, hard, and it went right toward him. But he didn't drop. The ball seemed to come to a complete stop. Alvin caught the ball!

"Unbelievable!" exclaimed Xander. "The chip-punk caught it! You're out, man," he said to Ryan gleefully.

"Dude's got hands," whispered Ryan to Xander.

"I think they're paws," corrected Xander.

"Whatever," said Ryan. "We could definitely use him on the team." He looked at Alvin in a whole new light.

When the class bell rang, Ryan approached Alvin. "Furball, I gotta say, you're good. Maybe you can hang out with us at lunch."

"The name's Alvin, and I've already got a table," responded Alvin.

Ryan nodded. "We'll save you a seat in case you decide to be popular."

"Right," said Alvin. "Like I'm going to leave my brothers."

Ryan shrugged and strutted off with his buddies. He knew a lot more about high school than Alvin did.

At lunch Alvin sat at the same table as the day before. Simon was playing chess with a member of the chess team.

He stroked his furry chin thoughtfully. "Hmm, quite a predicament," he mused out loud. "It seems you have me cornered. Or do you?" He picked up a chess piece and moved it across the checkered board. "Checkmate," he announced.

Simon noticed Ryan from across the cafeteria waving to Alvin. "Hey, Alvin," he said. "You're wanted at the jock table."

"Why would I go over there? Like I really need to worry about being popular. Hello, talking chipmunk, world famous rock star, guy with his own plush doll." Still, he couldn't hide it. He was looking longingly at the table where Ryan was sitting with his buddies.

Simon sighed. "Just go, Alvin."

"Yeah," added Theodore.

"You mean it? Thanks!" He leaped up and hugged Theodore and disappeared in an instant. Simon shook his head and popped a tater tot from Alvin's tray into his mouth.

Theodore sniffed. He smelled something interesting—and nice. He looked around the cafeteria and saw Emily, the girl he'd met yesterday. She was volunteering at the toy drive table and eating a piece of fried dough.

Theodore scampered over to her. In fluent Spanish he

told her that the churro smelled yummy.

Emily laughed. "Would you like a bite?" she asked.

"*¡Sí!*" answered Theodore.

"All right," agreed Emily playfully. "But only if you promise to bring a present." She pointed at the box.

Theodore promised that he would, again in Spanish, and placed his hand over his heart.

Emily was charmed and she handed over her churro to a delighted Theodore. He loved churros!

It turned out Toby had been right. The second day of school for The Chipmunks was a lot better than the first.

And with each day that passed Alvin became more and more popular. He lifted weights with Ryan and Xander—although his barbells were a little smaller than theirs. At lunch he showed off in front of the girls. Ryan would flip a grape into the air for Alvin to catch in his mouth. When the girls applauded, Alvin would invite them to call him on his cell phone.

After school, Alvin worked hard to impress his new jock buddies. When they burped too loudly or bragged about the classes they'd flunked, he laughed. Then he burped, too, and sang crazy songs about shaking his booty. It was great!

chapter 17

Ian and The Chipettes had moved into the vacant apartment, and Ian, still wearing his dirty bathrobe and ratty, old socks, was working hard to get the girls their first gig.

"I'm telling you," Ian said into a cell phone, juggling it with a coffee cup and a newspaper. "Alvin and the Chipmunks are old news. I have the next big thing. Singing *female* chipmunks!"

The phone went dead on the other end. No one was interested.

"What part of 'singing female chipmunks' don't you people understand!" screamed Ian to no one in particular. He trembled with rage and spilled his coffee—right onto the newspaper. That's when he spotted the headline about the school music competition. A music competition! That might be just the place to showcase The Chipettes!

"Girls!" he said to himself. "We're going to school!"

As usual, Alvin was sitting at the "cool" table. He could now catch grapes with eyes closed. After a particularly awesome catch, he and Ryan high-fived each other. That's when he saw Simon coming over.

"Hey, what's up, S?" he said. He tried to give Simon a fist bump, but Simon didn't respond.

"Don't leave me hanging, bro!" said Alvin, still holding out his paw.

Reluctantly, Simon knocked it. "Alvin, I know you've been busy with your buds, but I could really use your help at home."

"No can do," said Alvin, barely paying attention to him. "Ryan's going to teach me how to get pretty girls to do my homework."

"But you promised Theodore we'd hang out," pleaded Simon. "He misses Dave. And he misses you."

Alvin didn't want to hurt Theodore and whispered to Simon, "I can't."

"That's what you say every day," complained Simon. "Besides, it's your day to do laundry."

Ryan snickered. "You better listen to your daddy, Alvin. You don't want to be grounded." He tossed a balled-up napkin toward a garbage basket. He missed.

"Are you going to pick that up?" asked Simon, disgusted.

Ryan laughed. "Are you going to make me?"

"No," said Simon. "I'll just show you how it's done." He walked over and picked up the napkin and tossed it over his shoulder without looking—right into the garbage basket.

All the jocks at the table burst out laughing. Except Ryan. He was glowering.

"Ha! Ha!" said Alvin, seeing how mad Ryan was. "My brother. He's a real jokester. Always kidding. See you guys in class." He yanked Simon out of the cafeteria.

Alvin marched Simon down the hallway, furious. They passed Theodore, who was helping a bunch of kids hang posters about the music contest up on the walls. Theodore ran to catch up with Alvin and Simon.

"Why are you trying to embarrass me in front of my friends?" yelled Alvin to Simon.

"What?!" Simon was mad, too. "They're the ones you should be embarrassed by!"

Becca and Valentina, who'd been at their lockers,

noticed the boys and called out to them.

"Good luck with the show, guys," said Becca.

"Front row seats! I can't wait!" said Valentina.

There was nothing that Alvin loved more than fans. He wrapped an arm around each of his brothers as if everything were just fine between them.

"So what song are we going to sing?" asked Theodore. They hadn't practiced for the concert once. Alvin was too busy with his new friends.

"No pressure," said an unsmiling Simon. "But the whole school is counting on us."

"Oh, relax," said Alvin. "Like Ryan says, who's going to beat singing chipmunks?"

From behind an open locker door stepped Brittany.

Jeanette joined her.

Then Eleanor appeared.

Alvin and his brothers froze. Girl chipmunks. They were pretty—*really* pretty.

It was love at first sight. The boys couldn't take their eyes off the girls.

The school bell rang, and The Chipettes breezed past Alvin and his brothers. As soon as they were far enough away, however, they began madly whispering to one another.

"It's really them!" chirped Jeanette.

"Was Theodore looking at me? I think he was looking at me!" squealed Eleanor.

"Shh!" whispered Brittany. "You remember what Ian said. They can't be trusted."

Jeanette and Eleanor nodded. But it was going to be hard! In real life the boys were even cuter than they'd imagined!

chapter 18

Alvin, Simon, and Theodore were in the music room sitting on top of the piano. They were finally rehearsing for the big concert.

Julie Ortega, their teacher, was accompanying them on the piano. Dr. Rubin was thrilled as she listened to them. In the middle of one of their songs, however, their voices drifted off. All three boys had lost, dreamy looks on their faces.

"What happened?" asked Julie.

"Pink is my new favorite color," swooned Alvin, thinking of Brittany.

"Her glasses were quite fetching," gushed Simon, remembering Jeanette.

"She's like a beautiful green gumdrop," giggled Theodore, imagining Eleanor right in front of him again in her pretty outfit.

Dr. Rubin sighed. She'd worried about this when she'd admitted the girls to the school. "Maybe this is a good time for a break," she suggested. While Julie was distracted, Dr. Rubin took out her cell phone, ducked down next to the boys, and held out the camera phone. "For my screen saver," she whispered to The Chipmunks.

She smiled like a teenage fan and took the picture. But the moment Julie turned around, she straightened up and become the serious principal again.

Toby stuck his head into the music room. He'd come to pick up the boys after their rehearsal and had been waiting a long time. "Hey, guys," he called impatiently. "You ready to go? I've got a lot of important things to do at home."

"Like what?" teased Alvin. "*Not* make dinner?"

"That's cold," responded Toby.

Dr. Rubin walked over to Toby. "You must be the boys' guardian." She was looking him over. He seemed awfully young.

"Hi, Dr. Rubin. I'm Toby Seville. I graduated from here. Class of oh-two. You remember me."

Dr. Rubin wrinkled her forehead. She clearly didn't remember Toby, but she pretended that she did. "Oh. Yes.

Of course. You were in the same class as Miss Ortega, our music teacher now."

Julie stepped out from behind the closet door where she had been putting materials away. She hadn't seen Toby in eight years, but unlike Dr. Rubin, she remembered him. She smiled and waved excitedly. "Toby! Hi! It's been a long time."

Toby's eyes widened. He couldn't believe it. It was Julie. Julie. His high school crush. "Um, yeah, uh, you're looking . . . older." Why did he always have to feel like such an idiot around her? He pretended to check his watch. "Ooh! Look at the time. Guys, gotta go!"

He went to hurry out of the room, but walked in the wrong direction away from the door—and bumped into a bunch of music stands and instruments.

"Now I remember him," said Dr. Rubin.

"We will of course pay for those drums," said Simon.

"Anything for the school," added Alvin.

"The old false-modesty-suck-up routine. I remember it well," said a sinister voice.

It was Ian. He'd sauntered into the music room.

The Chipmunks couldn't believe it. They'd completely forgotten about Ian. Their jaws dropped. "Ian?!" they exclaimed.

"Mr. Hawke, can I help you?" said Dr. Rubin.

"In more ways than you know," said Ian smoothly. "I just heard about your music competition, and I skadoodled right down to see if I could volunteer my girls."

"Sorry, Mr. Hawke," said Dr. Rubin. "But I've already made my choice."

Ian smiled. "Maybe this will help you change your mind. Girls . . ."

Brittany, Eleanor, and Jeanette paraded into the room.

Alvin was shocked. "They're with *him*?"

Ian ignored Alvin and hit the play button on his boom box. Music kicked in, and the girls instantly launched into a highly polished musical number. They were fantastic!

Ian slithered over to the wall and turned the lights off and the PA system on. Now the whole school could hear The Chipettes! From the cafeteria to the gym, from art class to the tech room, kids came running to hear the fabulous singing. They crowded around the music room windows, peering in, listening and watching.

Ian had strapped flashlights to both knees, both elbows, his hands, and even his forehead, and was producing a homemade light show. And the girls were rocking! They were showstoppers!

"They're good," said Theodore, watching in disbelief.

"Good? They're killing!" enthused Simon. Alvin glared at them.

Ian leaned close to Dr. Rubin and shined all his lights on Brittany. "That one there?" he said. "Talent to burn."

The girls were taking their final bows and all the students were applauding. Julie and Toby were wildly clapping. Dr. Rubin tentatively joined them. She was clearly uncertain about what to do now.

Ian was studying Dr. Rubin very carefully. "So?" he asked, rubbing his hands together eagerly.

"Well," hesitated Dr. Rubin. "They were splendid. But as I said, I already made my decision."

"Whoa!" said Ian, getting a new idea. "Hold the phone, doc. *You* made the decision? It seems to me that this should be a *school* decision."

Alvin freaked out. "What?!"

"In the true spirit of democracy," continued Ian, ignoring him, "I say, let the people vote."

A cheer went up from all the students listening and watching. Dr. Rubin looked agonized. She just didn't know what to do. The Chipettes were such good singers. But so were Alvin and his brothers!

Ian went for broke. He said, "Let freedom ring, Dr. Rubin."

Dr. Rubin took a deep breath. In a way, Ian was right. "You make a persuasive case, Mr. Hawke. It's settled. This Friday, each group will perform one song in front of the student body. Whoever gets the most applause will represent our school."

The Chipettes were thrilled and began jumping up and down and clapping. Alvin and his brothers were shocked.

"When did this become a competition?" questioned Alvin.

"Ooh!" joshed Brittany. "Someone's afraid!" Ian nodded his head in agreement.

Alvin's striped face darkened. Something wasn't right here. No. There was something else going on. And he was going to find out what it was.

chapter 19

Brittany stood on the plastic lunch tray as it moved down the cafeteria line, gently pushed by the trays behind it. She already had a few tasty treats on her plate and was trying to decide what else she wanted. "Hmm," she pondered. "What else am I in the mood for?"

Alvin jumped up onto her tray beside her. "May I recommend a side order of advice?" he suggested suavely.

Brittany wrinkled her nose. "Now I've lost my appetite."

A lunch lady pushed a plate of wriggling gelatin onto the tray, which forced them to stand closer to each other—little black nose to little black nose. And they could both feel the chemistry. Brittany's eyelashes fluttered. Alvin's heart raced. After a beat, they pulled away from each other.

"I just wanted to warn you about Ian," said Alvin a little breathlessly.

"You should be grateful to Ian," scolded Brittany. "He did everything for you. And you broke his heart."

"First of all, he doesn't have a heart," answered Alvin. "And one of the things he did for us was put us in a cage."

"He'd never do that."

"Yeah," said Alvin. "'Cause you were there."

The lunch tray was getting closer and closer to the end of the line. "You better watch out," warned Alvin.

"I don't need advice from you," said Brittany, tossing her head. She thought he was talking about Ian.

"But . . . ," began Alvin, pointing over her shoulder.

"But nothing," interrupted Brittany. "Ian's taking u straight to the toooooppp!"

Her last word was lost as she toppled right to the bottom—of the cafeteria floor. Her food fell all aroune her. Alvin had jumped off the tray at the last moment "Got it," he said. "Straight to the top." He shook hi head. But at least now he had a better idea what Ian wa up to.

Out in the courtyard, Simon was playing chess b himself, moving from one side of the board to the othe

"You telegraphed that move," he said to his imaginary opponent as he pushed the chess timer.

In a different voice, he answered himself. "Or did I? The laugh's on you, my sorry little companion." He moved his queen across the board and quickly switched seats again.

Shyly Jeanette approached him. "May I sit here 'til recess is over?" she asked.

Simon blushed. "Don't you want to be with all your friends?"

"I don't really have any," answered Jeanette with a shrug and a smile. She looked at the chessboard carefully, her brown eyes narrowing. "You might want to move that rook." She pointed to the black chess piece.

Simon studied the board, nodding, and then carefully followed her advice. He jumped over to the other seat and began planning his next move.

Jeanette sighed. "If I want to fit in here, I have to act and dress like everyone else." She shook her head as Simon put his hand on his knight. "Might want to move the bishop," she suggested.

Simon's eyes widened as he thought about the move. He smiled at Jeanette and slid the bishop diagonally across the board. "Well, I'm in no position to give advice, but maybe it takes time to find your people, your group, your authentic friends. You know, your tribe."

In a very quiet voice, without meeting Simon's eyes, Jeanette whispered, "Maybe you would like to be in my tribe." Her glasses slid off her face to the ground and, as she reached down to pick them up, so did Simon. Their paws briefly touched.

"I'd be honored to be in your tribe," said Simon gallantly.

As they stood up, their heads bumped into each other. "Ow, sorry." Jeanette blushed.

"No, I'm sorry," said Simon, as embarrassed as she was.

The two chipmunks giggled nervously. "Good luck tonight," said Jeanette.

Simon nodded. He already felt like he'd had the good luck. Jeanette was so pretty. And she really knew how to play chess.

chapter 20

That night, Ian, wearing a tiny T-shirt and ballet tights, made The Chipettes practice their music routine over and over again. They were lined up in dance formation.

"We are so going to destroy those Chipmunks," bragged Brittany, still remembering everyone laughing at her in the cafeteria.

"That sounds mean," said Jeanette.

"They don't seem that bad," added Eleanor.

"Look," interrupted Ian. "If that's how you two feel, maybe we should withdraw from the contest. I'll pop you back into an express mail pouch and ship you back to whatever tree you came from."

Startled, the girls exchanged worried glances. That was the last thing they wanted.

Ian smiled sweetly, too sweetly. "Okay then. From the

top. And a one and a two and a three! Whoa! Short girl in the green. What's your name again?"

"Eleanor." Her face fell with disappointment. How come Ian couldn't remember her name?

"Right," said Ian without a trace of kindness. "I'm losing you back there. Have you always been that short?"

"I guess so," said Eleanor quietly.

"Yeah, you've got to work on that," he said. "And I want to try something here."

He motioned for Brittany to step in front of the others. Jeanette and Eleanor looked a little hurt.

Ian nodded his head, pleased. "This I like. And it's certainly not because Brittany is more of a super ultra mega star than you guys. . . ." He motioned for Brittany to step even farther away from the girls. "Great. Watch me now."

Ian launched into some ridiculous dance moves, and bravely, the three girls tried to imitate him.

chapter 21

Alvin, Simon, and Theodore cuddled under a blanket on their favorite chair watching the meerkat show. Theodore, in particular, was enthralled by the happy family antics. The narrator was describing how the little meerkat pups all worked together to dig out the dirt at the entrance to their burrow. "The meerkats huddle together at the end of a traumatic day to reaffirm their family bond. It's all for one and one for all. The Whiskers are going to have to rely on one another more than ever," said the television narrator.

This seemed like as good a time as any to bring up something that had been bothering Simon. "So, Alvin," he began carefully. "It's a funny thing today. We were one chipmunk short at rehearsal."

"I was busy," said Alvin. "Ryan and I . . ."

"Stop right there! If we're going to win the contest, we need you at rehearsals," said Simon.

He pulled the blanket closer and uncovered Alvin. Alvin pulled his share back and in seconds they were involved in a tug-of-war. Poor Theodore was caught in the middle. He just wanted to watch his show.

"Relax," said Alvin. "We're not going to lose. Now stop hogging." He yanked on the blanket.

"I'm not hogging," insisted Simon. He yanked back at the blanket.

"I think I'll sleep in my own bed tonight!" said Alvin.

"Ditto for me!" yelled Simon.

They jumped off the chair, leaving Theodore all by himself. He sighed sadly. He felt so alone these days.

A little while later, he crept into Dave's bedroom and crawled under the covers next to Toby. His whiskers tickled Toby's face. "Uh, Toby . . . can I sleep with you?" he whispered, even as he snuggled close.

"Uh, sleep with me?" asked Toby blearily. He rubbed his eyes.

"Dave let me."

Toby hesitated.

"My brothers are fighting," Theodore explained. He looked absolutely heartbroken, and Toby realized there was no way he could resist him.

"Uh, okay," Toby finally agreed. "Sure. Why not?"

Theodore smiled and hopped right up on top of Toby's face and curled up to go to sleep.

"Okay," said Toby, his words muffled by fur. "You're on my face. That's cool. I'm fine. This is what Dave would do. Um, your tail is in my . . ."

But it was too late. Theodore was already snoring.

chapter 22

Toby was having a nightmare.

In it, he was standing onstage with a blinding spotlight in his face. He couldn't see anything as he peered into the audience. All around him was a sea of black. Suddenly a single light shined on a girl sitting in the center of the front row. She was smiling at him, waiting for something. It was Julie. The Chipmunks' music teacher. Toby's high school crush.

Toby began to sweat. A lot. Almost paralyzed by fear, he awkwardly raised the microphone to his lips. "Um . . . ahh . . . err . . . uh . . ." No words would come out.

Julie was pointing at him, he now realized. Something was the matter. Toby looked around but couldn't see anything. And then he looked down. And he didn't see anything either. He didn't see his pants. All his clothes were gone and he was standing onstage in only his underwear.

The audience was roaring with laughter.

It was too much. Toby fainted and fell off the stage.

That's when he woke up, and snapped upright in bed. The sudden action sent the chipmunk, who had still been sleeping on his face, flying across the room. He thumped against the far wall.

"Where are my pants? I need my pants!" yelled Toby, utterly confused.

Theodore was confused, too. "I didn't do anything with them," he said.

Toby fell back on his pillows, and Theodore slowly crawled back into bed. He hoisted himself up the sheets and snuggled deep under the covers. A moment later, Toby passed gas and Theodore struggled to escape. It was stinky under there. Theodore was gasping for fresh air and that's when he saw them. The pants. "There's your pants, Mr. Stinky," he said to Toby.

But Toby was fast asleep.

chapter 23

Julie was organizing the toy drive in the music classroom. Emily and some of the other girls were wrapping boxes filled with toys.

"Thanks for chipping in today, guys," said Julie encouragingly. "This is a wonderful cause."

Theodore was trying to help. He stuck a bow on a small bicycle. But he looked glum.

"What's wrong with Theodore?" whispered Julie to Emily.

Emily shrugged. She didn't have any idea, but Julie noticed that another girl was looking just as sad and lonely as Theodore. It was Eleanor.

Julie smiled to herself. "Eleanor, perhaps you and Theodore could wrap presents together," she suggested.

Eleanor instantly brightened, but she didn't know

if she should. After all, Ian had told them so many bad stories about the brothers. But Theodore was shyly staring at her, and she couldn't resist. "Well, okay," she agreed.

Theodore gave her a huge smile and she smiled right back. She wobbled over to him as fast as she could, but she was having a hard time walking wearing the new ridiculously high platform shoes that Ian had given her.

"They don't look comfortable," commented Theodore.

"They're not," admitted Eleanor. "But Ian says I need to work on being taller." She teetered, lost her balance, and fell. Theodore rushed over to help her up.

"I think you look great just the way you are," he said to her.

"You do?" Eleanor smiled again. Theodore was so nice.

chapter 24

Out in the school courtyard Simon was playing chess—alone again.

Suddenly, a gust of wind blew a candy wrapper onto the board and knocked over one of the chess pieces. Simon picked up the wrapper and tossed it into a nearby trash can. Jeremy Smith, a tall handsome senior, watched him doing it.

"That's what we like to see," said Jeremy. "Responsible students putting litter in its place." He held out his hand as he introduced himself. He said he was the student body president.

"I'm . . . ," began Simon.

"International recording star and litter monitor Simon Seville." Jeremy laughed.

"Litter monitor?"

"Litter monitor," repeated Jeremy. "It's a new position we've created to help raise awareness about a pressing problem in our society."

"I couldn't agree more!" said Simon.

"Simon, I know it's a lot to ask, but we're looking for a take-charge guy to take charge of this very rewarding position. What do you say?"

Simon smiled. It was an offer he couldn't refuse.

Later that day he patrolled the cafeteria, holding an official-looking citation pad. He was supposed to write down the names of students who littered. He passed a table of kids. The table was clean and so was the floor. "Excellent job," he announced, nodding his head. "Gold stars all around."

The kids seemed kind of confused. A few of them even snickered, but Simon didn't notice as he moved on to the next table. There he noticed a candy wrapper on the floor. He pointed it out. "You probably weren't aware that you dropped a wrapper on the ground, so let's just call this a warning," he said to the kids at the table.

Again, the kids looked at one another surprised. When Simon moved on, they started giggling and pointing. At the "cool" table, Ryan, his buddies, and Jeremy laughed hysterically at the prank they'd played on Simon. They couldn't believe he'd fallen for it. Alvin arrived at the table just as they'd all begun talking about it.

"Hey, everyone," said Ryan. "Look who's here. The newest member of the football team."

"Really?" said Alvin, stunned.

"I talked to Coach," bragged Ryan. "You're in." There were high fives all around and Alvin started throwing pretend passes.

"So check it out, A-man," said Xander. "We're watching the new litter monitor." He pointed to Simon, who was just then writing up a student for dropping something on the floor.

Alvin was so embarrassed, he couldn't believe it. "I didn't know the school had a litter monitor," he mumbled.

"We don't," laughed Ryan. "But don't tell him that." Ryan picked up an empty milk carton and tossed it onto the floor. Alvin cringed.

"Are you going to pick that up?" asked Simon, coming over.

"Nope," said Ryan defiantly.

"I'm sorry to hear that," said Simon, shaking his head. "I'm going to have to write you a citation." He hopped up on the table to hand it to Ryan.

Ryan crumpled up the piece of paper and threw that on the floor, too.

Simon was angry. "You wanna play this game? I can play all day long."

"Simon," pleaded Alvin, trying to get his brother to stop.

"It's a joke, dude!" said Ryan.

"Litter is no joking matter," said Simon.

Everyone was laughing now at how seriously Simon was taking all this. Alvin was getting more and more uncomfortable.

"No, you're the joke!" teased Ryan. "We're messing with you! There's no such thing as a litter monitor."

"What?" Simon was confused. He looked down at his pad. He looked up at Jeremy, but Jeremy wouldn't meet his eye.

"It's true," said Alvin sadly.

"Alvin!" yelled Simon. "You knew about this? Does the word *brother* mean anything to you?"

"Yeah, well, Alvin's got some new brothers now that he's on the football team," said Ryan.

Alvin fidgeted and smiled nervously. He didn't want to do or say anything that would jeopardize his standing with the cool kids or his place on the football team.

Simon was heartbroken, but he didn't walk away. He stood his ground. "You still haven't picked up that litter," he said to Ryan.

"You want to get rid of litter?" laughed Ryan. "Let's start with you!" And Ryan picked up Simon just like that and tossed him into a deep garbage can full of lunchtime trash. The jocks cracked up, but Alvin felt terrible for Simon.

When the bell rang for the next class, he told the guys to go on without him, waited until they were all gone, and then hurried over to the garbage can. A janitor was carrying it out to the Dumpster. "Simon!" shouted Alvin.

He bolted across the cafeteria, but it was too late. The janitor had poured the garbage can into the Dumpster. A moment later, Simon's head, covered in trash, popped up over the rim. He stared at Alvin, surprised to see him still there.

"Okay, I'm a jerk," admitted Alvin. "Let's just get it out there. Are we cool?" He reached down to pull Simon up and Simon grabbed his hand—and yanked Alvin into the trash right beside him.

Garbage flew into the air as the two chipmunk brothers wrestled and fought. Finally, they both emerged from deep beneath the trash, breathless and exhausted.

"Alvin," gasped Simon. "Let's just put this behind us, for Theodore's sake. You know he's hanging by a thread."

"I know," panted Alvin, agreeing. "That's why I'm giving you the Alvin guarantee that I will be at the contest tonight."

Simon's eyebrows wrinkled. He was confused. "Why wouldn't you be there?"

"Because I . . . ," stumbled Alvin. He realized he hadn't said a word to Simon about his plans. "Because I have a football game," he finally mumbled.

Furious, Simon jumped on Alvin again, knocking them both back into the trash. Fur and garbage went flying.

"Simon? Alvin?" Theodore had come into the cafeteria wondering where his brothers were.

Alvin and Simon peeked over the metal rim of the Dumpster.

"Is everything all right?" asked Theodore, looking worried. His brothers were completely covered in trash.

"Absolutely, Theodore," lied Simon, trying to smile. He didn't want to worry Theodore.

"Couldn't be better!" agreed Alvin, trying to look relaxed. Awkwardly he put his arm around Simon.

Simon forced a smile. "We're like a couple of meerkats in here. All happy and peppy."

Theodore bought it. Relieved, he left the cafeteria to go back to class.

Simon turned on Alvin the moment Theodore was gone. "Do not miss that show," he ordered.

"I'll be there," said Alvin, not sure how he would. "Trust me."

That afternoon Theodore returned to the cafeteria by himself to hunt for a little treat for a hungry chipmunk. Just as he hopped up on the food counter, however, he heard Ryan and Xander approaching.

"It's too late for there to be any food left," Xander was saying as he sauntered into the cafeteria.

"I tell you there's always rice pudding left," said Ryan.

Quickly Theodore glanced at the bowls behind him and got an idea. Brothers had to stick up for brothers after all. Without another thought, Theodore added a special chipmunk "raisin" to the top of one of the puddings. At least, it looked like a raisin. Theodore jumped behind the counter as the two boys approached.

"Look, they finally got raisins!" exclaimed Ryan as he came near the food counter. He looked pleased. He dug a spoon into the pudding. "Mmm. Tastes a little funky, but I like it."

Hidden behind the counter, Theodore smiled. Revenge was sweet.

chapter 25

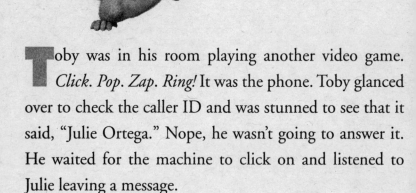

Toby was in his room playing another video game. *Click. Pop. Zap. Ring!* It was the phone. Toby glanced over to check the caller ID and was stunned to see that it said, "Julie Ortega." Nope, he wasn't going to answer it. He waited for the machine to click on and listened to Julie leaving a message.

"Hi, Toby. This is Julie Ortega. We talked yesterday. Well, we kinda sorta did. Anyway, the reason I'm calling is that I'm worried about Theodore. He's been acting a little down lately."

Toby was surprised to hear this and found himself worried about the little guy.

Julie's voice continued on the answering machine. "I hope you're going to the competition tonight. With his dad gone, Theodore needs all the support he can get. So

I'll see you there. Hope we get a chance to talk. Bye."
Click. She hung up the phone.

Toby felt awful. What could he possibly say to Julie? He always messed up when he was around her. He was dreading the concert.

Out on the football field the marching band was playing and the cheerleaders were waving a giant SCREAMING EAGLES banner. Alvin burst through the banner, creating a tiny hole. Moments later the rest of the team, led by Ryan, crashed through as well. Their huge bodies in all kinds of heavy football gear raced out, but tiny Alvin lead the way.

In the school auditorium everyone was excited, ready for the face-off between the two bands. Some kids chanted, "Chipmunks! Chipmunks!" and others sent out rousing cheers for The Chipettes.

Toby waited backstage with Theodore and Simon. He scanned the crowd. "I want you guys to know that I'm here for you tonight. I know I'm not Dave, but in a pinch, I think I can be Dave-ish."

This made Theodore feel better. It really did. He smiled at Toby.

Toby continued looking around nervously. There

she was. Julie. Their eyes met across the stage. Julie immediately smiled at him. Toby mustered a feeble wave in response, and vanished.

Onstage, Dr. Rubin approached the podium. She held up her hands to quiet down the rowdy crowd. "Welcome to our exciting sing-off between The Chipmunks and The Chipettes!"

Everyone applauded wildly and Dr. Rubin continued. "Remember students . . ."

There are no winners and losers tonight, Ian mouthed the all-too familiar words of teachers and parents everywhere. He rolled his eyes. "I'll remind The Chipmunks of that after we blow them off the stage."

"The band you choose tonight could give our school a chance to win twenty-five thousand dollars and save our music department," Dr. Rubin reminded the students. "So, without further ado, The Chipettes!"

The audience leaped to its feet, roaring with applause. Backstage, the girls prepared for their entrance. Eleanor held the microphone.

"Can you believe it, girls?" squealed Brittany.

But just as they stepped out onto the stage, Ian appeared. "Woah!" he called, stopping them. He grabbed the microphone away from Eleanor and tossed it to

Brittany. She was unsure at first, but Ian gave her a thumbs up.

Eleanor and Jeanette exchanged hurt looks, but what could they do right now? They still had to sing even if Brittany's voice was going to be the main one everyone heard. Brittany stepped out in front of her sisters and began belting out the song. She owned the stage. She was a diva.

Ian happily recorded the act on his cell phone.

Watching the amazing performance, Simon was worried. He paced back and forth wondering if they could possibly be as good as The Chipettes—especially without Alvin.

But Theodore was hopeful. "Don't worry, Simon," he said soothingly. "He'll be here."

Simon checked his watch. He just wasn't sure. If only he could really trust Alvin to be true to his word. Where was he?

At that exact moment, Alvin was sure he could finish the game and make it in time for the concert. The scoreboard showed only thirty seconds remaining in the fourth and final quarter. But the West Eastman Screaming Eagles were losing 28 to 24.

The whistle blew, and Ryan emerged from underneath

a pile of players from the opposing team. He glanced at the scoreboard, looked to the sidelines, and signaled his coaches with a hand gesture that looked like the letter *A*. Alvin. The coaches nodded, uncertain how one little chipmunk, no matter how good, could make any difference at this point.

Ryan huddled with his teammates. "It's time for the big 'A,'" he told them.

Alvin scurried over and the football players looked down. "Are you sure about this?" asked Xander.

Ryan nodded. He looked surprisingly confident. "Fourth and ten, Xan, we need to go with the secret weapon." He laid out his plan. "Twins right. Alvin left. Motion on me. Time to make history. Ready! Break!"

The offense came up to the line with Ryan at the lead. He took a good look at the other team's defense. Alvin moved far left as wide receiver. The defensive back facing Alvin laughed out loud. A chipmunk! How ridiculous. He didn't even need to cover this tiny dude. Or so he thought.

Ryan called out and lifted his foot ever so slightly to signal that he was about to move. "A-forty-two. A-forty-two," he signaled.

Alvin heard him and jogged toward Ryan before the

snap. Ryan hiked the ball, the defensive linemen collided, and Alvin disappeared beneath the shuffle.

Ryan dropped back, the football in his hands, and even though no receivers were open down field, he threw the ball anyway. It seemed like he was just letting it fly through the air to no one in particular.

The crowd groaned. How could he?

The ball flew toward the turf in the end zone with a spinning Alvin clutching the ball. Somehow, twisting and turning, clutching the ball the whole time, he managed to ensure that his feet hit the ground before the ball did. With a *thud*, he skidded to a stop underneath the ball.

Alvin raised the ball overhead so the referees could see. It was a touchdown!

Nobody could believe it. All eyes were on the referees. Would they let it stand? They would! West Eastman had won the game! The crowd went nuts.

Alvin celebrated with a touchdown dance at the goalposts. His teammates stampeded the field and mobbed him. Ryan picked up Alvin and held him over his head in triumph. "Who's the 'munk?! You're the 'munk!"

"Oh, yeah!" said Alvin.

"Alvin! Alvin! Alvin!" chanted the crowd. He was a hero.

chapter 26

Backstage, an increasingly irritated Simon kept checking his watch. Even Theodore was worried now. Toby ducked out from behind a curtain where he'd been hiding since spotting Julie.

"Where've you been?" asked Simon.

Toby lied, badly. "I was, uh, doing a perimeter check for Alvin. I looked in every nook and cranny but, uh, nothing."

Even Theodore didn't believe him.

The girls were finishing their number and bowing. Dr. Rubin, applauding, approached the podium again. "Super fantastic, girls!" she complimented them. "And now, let's hear it for the band that can rock you like a hurricane!" She stopped herself. She realized she shouldn't let the kids know which singers she preferred. "At least, that's what

I've been told. Here they are! The Chipmunks!"

The crowd applauded and cheered. But the stage was bare. No chipmunks appeared. Simon and Theodore weren't moving. Not without Alvin. Dr. Rubin, concerned, looked over to the wings.

Ian slid over to Simon and Theodore. "They say there's no *I* in *team*, but unfortunately for you, there *is* an *I* in *Alvin*," he said with smug satisfaction.

"Let's try again," said a hopeful Dr. Rubin. "Here are The Chipmunks!"

But again nothing happened.

"What should we do?" Theodore whispered to Toby.

Toby threw up his hands and shrugged. "I would . . . ask somebody who's not me."

Grimly Simon made a decision. He grabbed Theodore's paw and trudged out onto the stage with his brother. Confused, Dr. Rubin held out the microphone to Simon. He took it, but he just couldn't do it. He apologized to the crowd. "We've never performed without Alvin before, and we're not starting now."

The crowd sat in stunned silence for a moment and then began to boo.

Theodore leaned in close to the microphone. "You can't have two little pigs. You can't have two Musketeers.

And you can't have only two Chipmunks," he explained. His lower lip quivered. He looked like he was about to cry.

The audience couldn't believe it. No Chipmunks? It couldn't be.

Simon and Theodore retreated to the wings, and Toby led them away. He felt their heartbreak. He'd been there.

Even Brittany, Eleanor, and Jeanette looked upset and sympathetic. After all, The Chipmunks had been their inspiration.

Only Ian wasn't disappointed. As the crowd booed, he cupped his hand to his ear, enjoying the sound. "You hear that, girls? That's the sound of success."

Dr. Rubin was heartbroken, and she couldn't hide her feelings this time. "Well, that has to be a disappointment for all Chipmunks fans. So that means The Chipettes will represent West Eastman at the competition. Congratulations, girls."

Ian pulled the girls onstage for a celebratory bow and the audience went crazy.

But The Chipettes weren't happy. This wasn't how they had imagined their success.

chapter 27

Alvin was running as fast as he could to the auditorium. He yanked on the doors, but they were locked. Suddenly one of the doors flew open, almost knocking him over. Ian and The Chipettes rushed past Alvin.

"Life is good when you're not the loser," gloated Ian.

Alvin peeked into the auditorium. It was empty now. He was too late. He'd blown it.

Brittany had come back, telling the others she'd forgotten something. She came up close to Alvin. "You know," she told him, "your brothers were really hurt."

Alvin hung his head in shame. "They're never going to forgive me."

"You better find a way," scolded Brittany. "Because right now that *A* stands for . . ." She searched for the right word. " . . . stupid."

Brittany started to leave, then turned back to Alvin, and added, "Oh, and just so you know, this wasn't the way I wanted to win."

She scampered off and left Alvin alone with his thoughts in the empty auditorium.

Alvin walked home on his own and entered the apartment that night as quietly as he could. Alvin called for his brothers, but there was no answer. It seemed like everyone was already asleep. . . .

Simon and Theodore were just pretending to sleep with their heads turned away from Alvin. They were too upset, too disappointed.

"Guys? Guys?" tried Alvin.

But there was no answer. Theodore tried to hold back his tears.

chapter 28

A glow from the television screen came from the bedroom. Toby was playing virtual tennis. When the phone rang, he answered it, out of breath. "Hello?"

It was Dave—from Paris.

He was still all wrapped up in bandages and casts, but he was worried about his boys. "Toby? What are you doing at the house?" He was surprised to hear the voice of his irresponsible cousin.

"Playing tennis," said Toby lightheartedly. He picked up the controller and hit another ball coming at him on the screen. It was in! "I'm up three-one in the third set. My backhand is on fire." He slammed the ball across the net. In again!

"Where's Aunt Jackie?" asked Dave, the concern in his voice rising.

"The hospital," said Toby casually. "There was an, um, incident. Don't worry, she'll be out in a few weeks." *Slam!* His serve was really good these days.

"Toby?!" screamed Dave over the phone. "Who's watching the boys?"

"I am," answered Toby. He lunged to the right and whacked at another video tennis ball. "Before you freak out, they're doing great . . . ish."

Dave was panicked. Absolutely panicked. "What do you mean by 'ish'?"

Uh-oh! Toby realized what he'd said. He stopped playing video tennis and tried to backpedal. "Nothing! I mean, it's not like they're fighting or not being nice to one another. Because they are. Not the fighting part. The being nice part. All day long it's like, 'I love you, man' and 'You're the best brother ever.' It's kind of sickening, you know?"

There was a long pause on the other end of the line. Finally, Dave confronted Toby. "Toby, what is going on?"

"Hey, I know you're not supposed to be stressed so I'm going to go. It's all good here. Come home soon!" He hung up the phone as fast as he could. Whew! That was close. Now it was time to get back to his tennis game.

But Dave was frantic. He knew something was really

the matter. In a worried frenzy, he started hitting every button on his hospital bed. The sling holding his leg started to rise higher and higher and higher—until Dave was hanging over the bed, completely upside down.

"Nurse, nurse!" screamed Dave. "Get me out of here. I've got to get home to my boys."

chapter 29

When Ian got back from the competition that night, he immediately began sending the cell-phone video of The Chipettes to every music agency he knew. The sound wasn't great, the picture was a little blurry, but no one could deny that The Chipettes were absolutely incredible.

The very first music agent who saw the act had his assistant call Ian as fast as she could. These girls were going to be stars!

Ian was delighted to give The Chipettes the news. The next morning, while the girls were getting ready for the school performance, Ian told them that they were going to open that very night at a huge stadium. "There you are, my little moneymakers," he said. "Remember how I said I'd make you a star?"

The girls were shrieking and screaming with excitement.

"This is amazing!" squealed Brittany.

"Tonight?" realized Jeanette. "But we'll miss the big school contest."

"You're so smart." Ian smiled. "I don't have to explain anything to you. Obviously this was never about the school. It was about making Britt a star."

He pulled out three dresses—two were silver and one was sparkling gold. Ian held up the gold dress in front of Brittany, admiring how it was going to look on her. Jeanette and Eleanor couldn't hide their disappointment.

"That's what you wanted, right?" said Ian to Brittany.

"Uh . . . yes . . . but . . . ," stammered Brittany. She wasn't sure anymore. This wasn't right somehow.

"Well then, tonight's your chance. It's all you, Brittany."

"What about Jeanette and Eleanor?"

Ian shrugged. "They're backup."

Jeanette looked hurt. "But we're her sisters."

"We sing together or not at all," chimed in Eleanor.

"Fine," said Ian calmly. "Have it your way. Don't sing. All I need is Brittany here."

Brittany took a deep breath. She knew what she had

to do. "Ian, I won't do it without them."

"Wow," whistled Ian, his eyes narrowing. "That is so moving. Okay, Plan B. Do you guys like barbecue?"

The girls looked at one another. This all seemed too easy. But they nodded in answer to Ian's question. After all, they did *love* barbecued vegetables.

"Excellent!" Ian clapped his hands. "Because I know a great barbecue place that does an awesome chipmunk kebab." He smiled wickedly at the girls. "Unless of course, you'd rather sing."

Jeanette and Eleanor's eyes widened. Brittany gulped. They were in way over their heads with Ian. But what could they do now? They were trapped.

chapter 30

When Alvin woke up the next morning, the first thing he promised himself he'd do was apologize to Theodore. But Alvin couldn't find him anywhere. He wasn't in his bed. He wasn't in the kitchen. "Theodore?" called Alvin. "I don't blame you for being mad. . . ."

On the refrigerator was a note sloppily written in crayon. *I ran away from home. Don't look for me at the zoo 'cause I'm not there.*

Alvin raced to the zoo as fast as he could.

Theodore was so lonely. Not only did he miss Dave, but he also missed being a family. That's why he went to see the meerkat exhibit at the zoo. The meerkats he'd seen on television knew how to look out for one another.

But the meerkat exhibit was closed. A sign on the cage read VISIT OUR NEW EXHIBIT—BIRDS OF PREY. Only

Theodore didn't see the sign. He just climbed up on the cage and peeked through the bars, hoping to see some familiar friends. "Hello? Meerkat family? Hello?"

Maybe they were sleeping since it was still so early in the morning, he thought. Seeing and hearing no one, Theodore tried to slip between the bars, but his plump rear end stopped him for a moment. He wriggled and tugged and finally managed to squirm inside the cage.

It was decorated to look like a sparse desert with a grass floor, wispy shrubs, and a tree that climbed to the top of the cage. Theodore wandered around looking for the meerkats.

"Is anyone home?" he called hopefully. "My name is Theodore. I'd like to be in your family." Theodore wondered if maybe the meerkats had all gone to the beach like the pups in the television show.

A long screech echoed from the top of the tree.

Theodore froze. He recognized that sound. Slowly, nervously, he looked up toward the top of the cage—and there, perched on a branch, was a giant eagle. Its cold yellow eyes were peering at Theodore.

"You're not a meerkat." Theodore gulped.

He didn't know what to do. If he moved an inch, the eagle would swoop down and turn him into breakfast!

Just then Alvin, Simon, and Toby arrived at the fence outside the cage.

"Don't move, Theodore!" yelled Alvin.

"No . . . problem . . . there," said Theodore slowly, staying as still as possible. He didn't even want his lips to move!

"Hang tight, little guy," said Toby. "We're going to get you out of there."

Alvin and Simon slipped through the fence and ran to the cage. Unable to follow, Toby began to scale the fence.

"Let's think about this, Alvin," panted Simon, who was racing behind Alvin. "Eagles are deadly. We need a carefully executed rescue plan."

Alvin slipped through the bars of the cage effortlessly.

Simon sighed. "Or you can just run in there like a maniac."

The eagle screeched again as Alvin inched toward Theodore. He tried to talk to the bird to distract it from his brother. "Hey, birdie, over here." He pointed to the letter *A* on his shirt. "*A* is for appetizer!"

The eagle swooped down and landed right in front of Alvin. The menacing bird peered at him through the narrow slits of his eyes.

"I get why you want Theodore," chatted Alvin,

stalling for time. "But I can't let that happen. He's my brother. Not that he'd know that because I've been such a jerk lately."

Alvin sighed and looked apologetically at Simon. "If anyone deserves to be eaten, it's me."

The words hit home for Theodore. In that moment he forgave Alvin everything. The two brothers smiled at each other lovingly.

Meanwhile, Simon tried to distract the eagle. "Over here, buzzard boy! You want a piece of me?"

But the ploy didn't work. The bird kept moving toward Alvin. "Run . . . Theodore . . . run!" he urged.

"I will!" promised Theodore—and he dashed as fast as he could right through the eagle's outspread legs and grabbed Alvin. "Let's go!"

The furious bird chased after the two chipmunks as they sprinted toward the bars. Theodore went to slip through, but he got stuck again! "Help, guys!" he called.

Alvin pushed from behind, while Simon pulled. The eagle was stalking them, moving closer and closer. Finally, with a squish and a plop, Theodore's plump backside made it through. And the bird swooped down just as Alvin followed his brother through the bars to safety.

"Dudes! That was huge!" Toby had finally managed to

climb over the fence and reach the cage.

"We all did it together!" beamed Theodore.

Alvin threw an arm around Simon. "You hear that? Together."

Simon paused, still unsure whether he was completely ready to forgive Alvin.

"C'mon, Simon, hug it out," prompted Theodore.

"Don't make me have to kiss you," said Alvin. "Because I'll do it. I'll plant one on you right now." He puckered up to Simon. "Here it comes."

Simon smiled despite himself. He blocked Alvin with his hand, laughing. "I think I'll take the hug."

The brothers embraced, and in an instant Theodore had joined them in their huddle. Toby watched, genuinely happy that they were reunited.

chapter 31

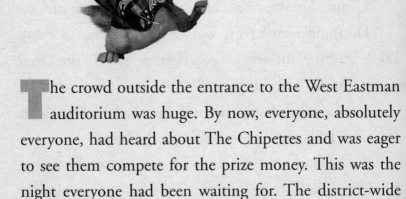

The crowd outside the entrance to the West Eastman auditorium was huge. By now, everyone, absolutely everyone, had heard about The Chipettes and was eager to see them compete for the prize money. This was the night everyone had been waiting for. The district-wide music competition!

An emcee in a shiny suit with greased-back hair stepped onstage. "Welcome, everyone, to the renowned East Westman School!"

Someone quickly ran out onstage and whispered a correction to him.

"Oh," said the emcee. "I mean, West Eastman School. I'd like to thank all of you for coming out to support music in our schools. We've got a lot of acts, and the school has to turn off the heat at nine thirty, so without further ado, representing Orange Grove High, put your hands together for . . . Lil' Rosero!"

The crowd went wild. Backstage, Dr. Rubin and Julie clapped along with everyone else. The curtain opened to reveal an exciting hip-hop group that broke into an impressive song-and-dance routine.

Meanwhile, The Chipmunks and Toby had just arrived at the school to support The Chipettes. As they crossed the front lawn, Theodore saw the scary eagle statue that was the mascot of the school and jumped up on its arm. "What?! You want some?!" Theodore wasn't scared of eagles anymore—at least not pretend ones.

Toby's cell phone rang and he looked at it, surprised at the caller ID. "Ian Hawke?"

Alvin grabbed the phone from Toby. "I'll take that." Alvin pressed speakerphone. "What could you possibly want, lowlife?" said Alvin to Ian.

"Alvin?" It was Brittany.

"Oh," said Alvin, surprised. "Brittany."

"We're not going to be able to perform tonight. Could you guys fill in for us?"

"What about the music department?" asked Alvin. "The whole school is counting on you."

"I know," said Brittany, trying to hold back her tears.

"Oh, Alvin! I should have listened to you about Ian."

"Don't tell me . . . ," said Alvin.

"Yep," said Brittany. "He locked us in a cage." Back at the loft apartment, Ian had put the three chipmunks in a hamster cage with a lock. The girls had managed to snag Ian's cell phone through the bars with the help of Jeanette's glasses. Ian was busy arguing with a limousine driver about the kind of car he wanted.

Alvin took charge at once when he learned about this. He gave the phone to Simon so he could tell the girls how to pick a lock.

Toby shook his head. "I'll break the news to Dr. Rubin." He headed toward the auditorium.

Alvin was thinking, planning. "I need to get to the girls ASAP," he said.

"I know how!" announced Theodore. He whispered to Alvin his plan.

Alvin raced into the school. Moments later he reemerged—riding on the minicycle from the toy drive. In his hand were three tiny toy helmets.

Inside in West Eastman, Lil' Rosero was finishing its act. The crowd had loved it. Even outside, Simon and Theodore could hear the cheers. But they didn't let themselves be distracted. They had girl chipmunks to rescue.

"Okay, now just slowly turn your nail in the lock and wait for the click," explained Simon, talking the girls through their breakout.

"It clicked!" chirped Jeanette. "Gotta go. Ian's coming!" As quickly as she could, Jeanette used her glasses to push Ian's cell phone back to its original place.

"All right, girls," said Ian. "Time to get fabulous."

Ian was in his glory. He was riding in a limo with an act that would hit the top of charts. "Driver man," he ordered once he'd settled into the backseat, the cage at his side. "Take me to the stadium, pronto."

He leaned back in the leather seat and turned on the twinkling overhead lights. He adjusted the volume on the stereo and opened the moon roof. He noticed a bottle in the limo. "Ooh, a little bubbly. Don't mind if I do."

Ian reached for the champagne bottle cooling in a bucket, and while he was distracted trying to pop the cork, the girls made their move. Brittany quietly opened the cage door, and she and her sisters slipped out, scampering up through the moonroof without Ian noticing.

Ian was imagining his revenge when the cork popped. He poured himself a glass of champagne. "A toast," he smiled, holding the glass up to the cage. "To the ladies who will knock The Chip-chumps off the top."

But before he took the first sip, he noticed something. The cage was empty. The girls were gone! "Girls?! Girls?!" he called frantically.

He looked around the backseat. Nothing. He peered into the driver's seat. Nothing. He looked out the rear window—and he saw three furry butts sliding down the glass!

Ian jumped up and poked his head out through the moonroof. The Chipettes were balanced on the shiny trunk of the car, strapping on tiny crash helmets. "Where do you think you are going?"

That's when he saw Alvin weaving back and forth on his bicycle behind the limo. The girls leaped onto the bike and Alvin sped away, waving good-bye to Ian.

"ALVINNN!!" screamed Ian.

The cycle weaved between cars and veered abruptly around a corner.

Ian had the driver turn around, but the limo couldn't follow the tiny bike through the heavy traffic. Ian looked around and saw a toy store. He jumped out of the car and ran inside. A moment later he was back with a tiny remote-controlled helicopter in his hands.

Alvin and The Chipettes raced along a sidewalk toward the school. Overhead, a helicopter buzzed in hot pursuit.

Onstage at West Eastman an act from another high school was performing to wild applause. Backstage, Theodore and Simon were anxious. Would Alvin pull it off? Could he really rescue the girls? Would they make it back in time to compete for West Eastman?

"How are we doing?" asked Toby, stepping backstage.

"No word from Alvin," Simon informed him. He was more worried than ever.

The curtain closed and the emcee stepped in front of it. The audience was quiet as if everyone were holding their breath. This is what they had been waiting for all night! "And now the final act of the night," announced the emcee. "We've had a last-second change in the lineup but we don't think you'll be too disappointed. Representing West Eastman, it's The Chipmunks!"

The surprised crowd roared with approval. This was even better! The Chipmunks? They were celebrities!

Backstage, Theodore and Simon didn't know what to do.

The emcee waited. Nothing happened. He tried to announce the act again. "Like I said," he yelled in a louder voice toward the wings of the stage. "The Chipmunks!"

The audience began to chant, "Chipmunks! Chipmunks!"

"We have to go out there," said Simon.

"I don't want to be booed again," said Theodore.

Toby looked at their stricken faces. He couldn't let them fail. He just couldn't. And he wouldn't.

The emcee was getting impatient. "Well, if there are no Chipmunks, I guess we'll have to move on."

The crowd booed and then stopped. Out of nowhere, Toby had walked stiffly to the microphone. He made a gesture for the crowd to simmer down. Simon and Theodore looked on in shock. Out in the audience, Julie looked puzzled as well. What was Toby doing?

Toby could feel Julie's eyes on him, so he looked down at his shoes to avoid accidentally seeing her. "Hey, everybody," he said. "I'm Toby. The Chipmunks will be out very, very, very soon, I hope. Emphasis on *very soon*."

Theodore couldn't believe that Toby was helping them out. "Dude, this is huge," he whispered.

But when Toby glanced up at the audience, out of that sea of faces he saw Julie's. That was it. She did it every time. He froze up completely. He couldn't speak or move or do anything.

And where was Alvin? Doing his best to get to the school on time—dodging and weaving on the bike to avoid the helicopter. Ian was pressing the controller like a madman, and he couldn't believe it when he saw Alvin turn completely around and head right toward him. "That's right, Alvin," he said. "Bring my Chipettes to me!"

"Hold! Hold! Hold!" Alvin commanded the girls. "Now!"

Timing it perfectly, The Chipettes leaped up and grabbed the skids of the helicopter just above them. Alvin popped a wheelie and jumped up to join the girls. And the abandoned cycle was zooming right at Ian!

Only Ian didn't see it. He was looking at the helicopter, convinced he'd captured all The Chipmunks. Even as the helicopter soared up, he reached up and grabbed Alvin's dangling legs. "Ha! Got you!"

Boom! The cycle smashed right into Ian and sent him hurtling backward. The remote control flew up into the air. The helicopter began spinning out of control.

"We need the remote!" yelled Alvin.

"Got it!" said Jeanette. The remote control was in her paw. She was hanging upside down, her feet held by Eleanor, whose feet were held by Brittany, whose tail was held by Alvin. It was teamwork all the way!

But that didn't help poor Toby! He was still stuck onstage unable to speak. And the crowd was growing restless. "This is a music contest! We want music," heckled an audience member.

Simon and Theodore knew they had to do something. "We have to go out there," said Simon, resolved.

But at that exact moment Toby snapped out of his paralysis. Enough was enough. He knew what he had to do. He took a deep breath, wiped the sweat off his forehead, looked right into Julie's eyes, and began to sing.

"Ever since I met you, I wanted to be your guy," he crooned awkwardly. *"But, as maybe you've noticed, I'm pathologically shy. So maybe I'll start by saying . . ."* He paused and took another deep breath. "Hi." He waved at Julie.

And Julie waved back.

The crowd broke out into applause, and thinking it was for him, Toby took a bow. But the audience was cheering for the helicopter that had just zoomed through the ceiling window with four chipmunks—one of them holding a remote control in his paws.

Backstage, Simon and Theodore jumped up and down with happiness. "Alvin!"

The helicopter gently touched down on the stage. Theodore pointed to a backup band that began to play. A thrilled Dr. Rubin pumped her fist in the air.

Alvin helped the girls off the helicopter and handed Brittany the microphone. She immediately gave it to Eleanor and Jeanette and all three girls began to sing. After their first chorus, the boys joined in, harmonizing. The crowd was going crazy! Two chipmunk acts in one!

Dr. Rubin couldn't resist the music and started to dance—much to the surprise of the students and teachers.

Best of all, Toby, who had left the stage, approached Julie. A little nervous still but trying to hold on to his newfound bravery, he stuck out his hand for a handshake. Julie smiled—and wrapped her arms around him in a joyous hug.

The Chipettes and The Chipmunks were bringing down the house! These chipmunks could rock! And when their song had finally ended and they had taken bow after bow to a standing ovation, there was no question in anyone's mind about who had won the contest. The emcee walked out with a giant check made out to West Eastman and handed it to Dr. Rubin.

Talent and teamwork had saved the school's music program!

chapter 32

Across the city at the stadium another audience was waiting to see The Chipettes. The curtain parted, the crowd screamed, and a strange sock puppet peeked out.

"I'm Jeanette!" someone squeaked. A rough drawing of a chipmunk was taped to the puppet.

Another sock puppet poked out through the curtain. "I'm Eleanor!"

And then Ian parted the curtains and stepped out. The sock puppets were in each of his hands, and he was wearing a torn gold curtain as if it were a ball gown. He'd used a black marker to draw stripes on his face, and a tail made of old wigs poked out the back of the dress. "And we're The Chipettes!" Ian said in a high-pitched voice.

The crowd was dumbstruck. They'd paid money for this?

Ian began to sing tunelessly and move the puppets up and down as if they were dancing.

But the crowd had had enough. An angry wave of tween-age girls stormed the stage—and Ian disappeared beneath them.

Two large security guards marched up to the stage, pulled a dazed Ian from the angry mob, dragged him outside, and threw him into a Dumpster. Ian was right back where he started. Which was exactly what he deserved.

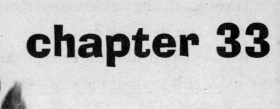

chapter 33

The crowd was going wild with all that music. Everyone was dancing, but Theodore noticed something else, someone hobbling and dancing on crutches at the back of the gym. "Dave!" he shouted.

The Chipmunks dashed across the stage and jumped onto Dave's shoulders. Alvin leaped up right onto the top of his head.

"We missed you!" chirped Theodore. "Did you get our card?"

"Still coughing up glitter," said Dave, smiling.

"So how much did you miss us?" asked Theodore, happier than he had been in weeks.

He cuddled up right next to Dave's ear.

"Probably quite a bit," said Simon sensibly, although he was also holding on to Dave as tight as he could.

"Of course I missed you. You're my boys." Dave smiled.

"Cool," nodded Alvin, beaming. "And sometimes boys make mistakes and break TVs."

"Alvin, what did you . . ."

"It doesn't matter," interrupted Alvin hastily. "We're together again! Reunited! Busta move, Dave!"

And Dave and his happy Chipmunks all began to dance together.

After the show, The Chipmunks and The Chipettes hung out on the stage watching the audience leave. Simon was surprised to see Ryan, Xander, and Jeremy grumpily picking up litter between the seats.

He turned to Alvin. "Did you have something to do with this?"

Alvin shrugged and smiled mischievously at Dr. Rubin.

Simon beamed. "Thank you, Alvin!"

"How ya feeling?" Simon asked Dave.

"Aside from this cast itching like crazy, I'm good."

"Got you covered, Dave!" said Alvin. He scurried down Dave's leg and stuck his little arm deep inside the cast and began to use his claws to scratch.

"Little to the left. Right there. Ahh!" Dave sighed. "I

gotta say, Alvin, I thought you were going to get into a lot of trouble. But I can see I was wrong."

"Trouble?" said Alvin innocently. "Me?" He glanced over at Simon and Theodore, who let him know that their lips were sealed.

"Let's not push it, Alvin," said Dave. "My point is, after what I saw tonight, I realize I got all worked up for nothing. I've got to start trusting you guys."

"Our thoughts exactly," said Simon.

"And who are these talented girls?" Dave had noticed The Chipettes.

"Dave, may I introduce Brittany, Jeanette, and Eleanor," said Simon gallantly.

"They're going to be staying with us for a while," said Theodore shyly.

Dave tried not to smile too much. "Of course they are. Okay, Alvin. That's enough. I think you got it."

Alvin tried to pull his hand out of the cast, but he couldn't. "It's stuck!"

"Ow!" yelled Dave. "That hurts. Don't you ever cut your nails?"

Alvin pulled harder but it was no good. He couldn't get his hand out. Toby and Julie came over to see what was going on.

"Hey, Dave, welcome back," said Toby.

"Toby, I'll be honest, when I heard you were going to be watching the boys, I had my doubts. Ow! Alvin!"

Alvin now had his feet on the cast and was using them for leverage as he pulled on his hand. Dave wriggled. It hurt—but he tried not to let Alvin know that. He turned back to Toby. "But, Toby . . . you look like . . . you were a . . . good influence on them."

Simon raised his eyebrows. "Good-ish."

Toby smiled sheepishly. "Actually, I think it was the other way around."

"Ow!" shrieked Dave again. "Alvin! Get your hand out of there!"

"I'm trying, Dave. I'm trying."

Dave balanced himself on his crutches and started shaking the leg with the cast on it, hoping to get Alvin off it. "Alvin! Please!"

"Stop moving, Dave!" begged Alvin, who was getting tossed this way and that.

With one final kick of his leg, Dave shook Alvin free—but he lost his balance and staggered backward, slamming into a stack of enormous speakers.

The speakers, balanced one on top of another in a giant tower, began to teeter and fall.

"ALVIN!!"

That chipmunk had done it again.

chapter 34

The three chipmunks were all tucked in, their covers pulled up to their furry chins. They were settled and happy. Dave was home. They were a family again.

"Look at you, already in bed." Dave smiled, shaking his head. "Looks like Toby was a good influence."

"Uh, yeah." Alvin held back a laugh. "Toby was great, but frankly, 'you're the man!'"

"You're the man!" joined in Simon and Theodore.

"Thanks, guys." Dave beamed. "Now, lights out. Good night, everybody."

"Good night, Dave!" chirped The Chipmunks.

"Good night, Dave!" said Theodore and Simon again.

Dave noticed the missing voice. "Alvin?" he questioned.

"I'm not tired!" said Alvin, jumping up.

"Sorry," answered Dave, shaking his head. "But you've

got school tomorrow." He hit the lights and the room went dark.

Just as Dave was shutting the door, he saw a little paw reaching up to switch the lights back on. "Come on, Alvin," he said in a serious voice. "Time for bed."

Dave shut the lights off. And grinning mischievously, Alvin turned them back on.

"Alvin, stop," said Dave. "It's late."

Dave turned the lights off. Again. Alvin turned the lights on. Again.

Dave lost it. "ALVIN!!" he yelled. The reunion was over, and it was just like old times. "Alvin! That's it! Don't make me come over there."

Dave turned off the lights one more time.

And this time they stayed off.

But just as Dave was marching out of the room, he stepped on Alvin's tiny skateboard. "Whoa!" he shouted, losing his balance. Dave flew up in the air and fell. "ALVIN!!"

Alvin turned on the lights. Dave was sprawled on the floor, out cold, and Alvin knew he was in trouble. Big trouble. Again.

Alvin pretended to yawn. "I am kind of tired after all. Good night, Dave," he whispered, and he shut off the light as fast as he could.